# WHILE MY HEART BEATS

# What Reviewers Say About
# Erin McKenzie's Work

**Where Love Leads**

"[F]antastic writing for a first book, and I cannot wait to see what McKenzie does next. If you love a feel-good romance that's built of more than just fluff, you definitely want to read this book."—*Rainbow Book Reviews*

"*Where Love Leads* is an enjoyable book, the characters well developed and the contrast between the fast and furious young love of Kat and Bridget and the slow smoldering mature looks of affection and understanding between Sarah and Lauren was wonderful."—*Lesbian Reading Room*

"Though this book touches on some tough subjects, there are plenty of heartwarming moments, and it speaks to the power of healing and surrounding one's self with supportive and loving people. I'd recommend it if you can handle the tougher parts. It's worth it in the end."—*Kissing Backwards*

# By the Author


Where Love Leads

Taking Chances

While My Heart Beats

# WHILE MY HEART BEATS

*by*

## Erin McKenzie

2020

# WHILE MY HEART BEATS

ISBN 13: 978-1-63555-589-9

This Trade Paperback Original Is Published By
Bold Strokes Books, Inc.
P.O. Box 249
Valley Falls, NY 12185

First Edition: May 2020

**Credits**
Editor: Ruth Sternglantz
Production Design: Susan Ramundo
Cover Design By Jeanine Henning

# Acknowledgments

Many thanks to the Bold Strokes team, whose professionalism and support are much appreciated. To my editor, Ruth—your encouragement and expertise mean the world to me, and I've become a better writer thanks to you. To my first readers—Tricia, Mary, and Sarah—thank you for your time and valuable input. To the many authors and readers I've met since I began this journey, you inspire me to keep writing, and you've enriched my life tremendously. Lastly, to my family—you give me your love, support, and the time and space to accomplish this writing thing. I couldn't do it without you, and I am deeply grateful. Love you to the moon and back.

# Dedication

This book is dedicated to the memory of the nurses and Voluntary Aid Detachment volunteers who gave exemplary service during World War I under difficult and dangerous conditions. Their acts of extreme bravery and compassion saved countless lives and forever changed the role of women in wartime. The impact of these largely unsung heroes was immeasurable, and I am proud to honor them.

## CHAPTER ONE

*October 1915*

Ellie watched the driving rain form rivulets on her bedroom windowpane, blurring the massive stone griffins that stood down below, guarding the manor's main entrance. It was a nasty day, but the foul weather did nothing to dampen her enthusiasm. She was off to join her friends today, but in truth she'd welcome any excuse to get out of the house and away from Mother's incessant nagging.

She stood before the gilded oval mirror, straightening the collar and smoothing the skirt of her emerald green dress, which showed a bit more ankle than her mother condoned. Violet Winthrop had chosen every bit of decoration that adorned the house, but Ellie drew the line at being another of Mother's ornaments. She pinned on her new velvet cartwheel hat at a jaunty angle that matched her rebellious mood. Smiling, she glanced around her bedroom, every ornate inch colored in shades of rose, ivory, and gold. Someday, she thought, she'd have her own home, and it wouldn't be quite so…pretentious.

She headed down the corridor and descended the wide marble staircase into the front hall. While pulling on her coat,

Ellie poked her head into the parlor. Her mother and younger brother were having afternoon tea.

"I'm heading into town for a bit. I expect to be home in time for dinner."

Mother was perched on the edge of the settee, her back ramrod straight, ever the proper English lady. She wore her second—or was it her third?—outfit of the day, a blush-colored dress with a high ivory lace collar that might have been a bit too tight, if the look on her face was any indication.

"For heaven's sake, Eleanor, why would you want to be gallivanting about in this weather? What's going on in town?"

"I'm meeting my friends for a little get-together." In fact, they'd begun meeting a few months earlier to discuss women's rights and the vote, despite the fact that wartime suffragist rhetoric had necessarily shifted to talk of patriotism and peace.

"Don't tell me you're still hanging around those rabble-rousers clamoring for women's rights. What a ridiculous waste of time."

Ellie couldn't help but rise to the bait. "The suffragists' cause is not ridiculous, Mother. Why shouldn't women be allowed to vote? This is our country, too."

"Well-bred and respectable young women should not concern themselves with such things. Your father has provided all you will ever need, and someday soon, God willing, a fine husband will do the same," Mother said. She nodded and looked away, as if the matter was settled.

"I say let the women vote," her brother said, his mouth full of cake. "Then when some dodgy MP gets in there and mucks things up, they can share the blame."

"Theodore, use your manners."

Theo swallowed his cake and grinned at Ellie.

"I just don't see why you would want to associate with such people, Eleanor," Mother went on. "Those so-called ladies we read about in the papers are nothing more than common criminals. What do you do at these get-togethers, exactly?"

"We sit in Katherine Piper's parlor, have tea, and talk. That's hardly a crime."

Mother sniffed. "I never liked that girl. Far too opinionated, if you ask me."

Theo snorted a laugh, nearly spilling his tea. Mother gave him a sharp look, and he coughed a couple of times, pointing to his throat.

"Wrong pipe."

*Bless you, little brother.* Ellie seized upon his diversion, needing to disengage before she lost her temper. "Let's agree to disagree, Mother. Bailey's got the car waiting, so I really must go. Have a lovely afternoon." She heard her mother grumbling as she hurried away.

Outside, the chauffeur stood beside the front entrance, umbrella in hand. He protected her from the rain as they walked to Papa's old Model T and held the door open for her.

"Thank you, Bailey. Please take me to Number Nine Pritchard Street."

"Very good, miss," he said, touching his cap. He cranked the engine and drove slowly down the long drive.

"Have you got errands in town while I'm visiting, Bailey?"

"Well, miss, if you think I'd have the time, I thought I might look in on my boy and his wife, now they've had their baby. The little lad is my first grandchild, you know."

"Oh, but of course you must, Bailey. Do give them my congratulations. What's the baby's name?"

"They've called him James, after me. Isn't that fine?"

Ellie could hear the pride in his voice, and she smiled. "Yes, it is. Take your time visiting, Bailey. As long as we're back before dinner, Mother won't fuss too much."

"Thank you, Miss Eleanor."

They rode on in silence, Ellie's thoughts turning to her impending visit. She was very interested in the idea of women's rights, and having other people to share that interest was wonderful. She'd certainly not have such discussions at home.

Eight young women had gathered at Katherine Piper's home, and the parlor was buzzing with chatter. Three-tiered serving plates were filled with sandwiches of smoked salmon, ham, or cucumber, cinnamon scones, and various tea cakes. The guests mingled and sampled the fare, sipping tea or raspberry cordial, until the hostess called the meeting to order. Ellie took a seat on a lovely blue velvet and mahogany armchair with her glass of cordial and turned her attention to Kate.

"Ladies, thank you for coming," Kate began. "For today's topic, I thought we might discuss what our roles should be in the ongoing fight for women's suffrage. There are many things we can do here in Surrey to give our support to the movement. I learned a great deal when I heard Emmeline Pankhurst speak in Manchester before the war. She was brilliant, I tell you. She doesn't stand by, quiet and meek, in the face of injustice."

"Maybe so," Helena said, "but setting fires and inciting violence isn't the answer, either. The suffragettes are making it more difficult for the law-abiding suffragists to be taken seriously. And what about those women who were force-fed in prison? How awful!"

"I agree," Ellie said. "Poking the tiger won't make him any less inclined to eat us."

Jeanne laughed. "So true. I say peaceful, intelligent conversation is the answer. True change takes time."

"How many men do you know who think women are capable of intelligent conversation?" Millie said. "My mother hasn't bothered to voice an opinion for years, just to avoid my father's condescending replies." She shook her head in disgust. "I tell them this is a quilting circle, so I don't have to listen to his nonsense about a woman's place and all that."

Jeanne looked sympathetic. "We'll never change everyone's mind, but some can be convinced, I'm sure."

"The war may be doing the convincing for us, in a way," noted Kate's cousin, Rose. "With so many men off fighting, Britain must rely on women to do what we've never done before. Women are building airplanes, and running their own hospitals, and driving ambulances in the war zone. Imagine what else we can do."

Ellie turned to see her friend leaning forward in her chair, her face alight with excitement. Rose usually didn't speak up at these meetings, as her cousin tended to demand the spotlight, and Ellie smiled at her enthusiastic conviction.

"Yes, Rose, that's all well and good for them," Kate said, "but not everyone is cut out for such labor. I for one prefer not to get my hands too dirty. Imagine what Jonathan would think if I had grease under my nails."

Rose blushed as the others laughed, and the conversation veered inexplicably to the topic of men. As much as Kate liked to talk about suffrage, Ellie suspected that she would run off and join the circus if her new beau asked. She wondered if the other girls were here because they wanted to be in Kate's inner circle, supporting her social cause du jour, or if they truly believed in the rights of women. She listened politely but wasn't the least bit interested in all the talk of the most eligible bachelors and how dashing they looked in uniform. Rose caught her eye and beckoned with a pat on the cushion beside her. As the others giggled and gossiped, Ellie joined her on the settee.

"Well, that didn't take long," Rose said, rolling her eyes.

"Which part? Kate pooh-poohing your idea or Kate gushing about Jonathan?"

"Both," Rose replied. "Thank goodness you don't go in for such drivel. I need a kindred spirit who can keep me company in moments like this."

Ellie laughed. "I'm happy to be of service. But really, Rose, why do you keep coming when Kate irritates you so?"

"Because my mother insists I get my nose out of my books and socialize. If I didn't come here, she'd find worse fates for me, like taking tea with dotty old Aunt Tillie, who smells funny and is always pinching my cheeks too hard."

Ellie giggled. "That sounds unpleasant."

"You've no idea. So you see, I'd much rather come to Kate's. I think she resents having to babysit me, but I can handle her. Plus I enjoyed the earlier conversation, short as it was."

"So did I, but our book chats are much more fun. You're the only person I know who reads as much as I do. Besides, all this talk of boys is tiresome. I know most of them anyway, and the majority are quite irritating."

Rose laughed. "How refreshing it is to hear you say that. My mother is constantly after me to tidy my hair or stand up straight, in case a young man happens by. She's even threatened to move us to London to increase my prospects. I'm only seventeen, for God's sake. It's maddening."

Ellie knew exactly how Rose felt. "Our mothers must be cut from the same cloth. Mine is forever saying, *How will you* *ever catch a husband if you...*blah-blah-blah. I'm sure you can fill in the blanks. My mother thinks I'm already past my prime and is mortified that I'm not yet married at my advanced age of twenty-two."

Rose widened her eyes and put her hand to her mouth in mock horror. "How perfectly dreadful!"

Ellie laughed. "What do you want, then, if it's not to catch a husband?"

"I want to teach literature. I'm particularly interested in feminist writings at the moment. It's refreshing to read about strong, independent women, rather than the weak, simpering ones who cannot function without a man."

Ellie's curiosity was piqued. "That sounds interesting," she said, "though I'm fairly certain I won't find anything like that in the library at home. If you're willing to lend me a book or two, I'd love to read them."

"Yes, of course. It would be wonderful to discuss them with someone who doesn't find the subject matter appalling," Rose said.

"Appalling? How so?"

"Well," Rose said, lowering her voice, "besides the headstrong women part, some of the writers refer to intimate partners of the same sex." Ellie couldn't hide her surprise, and Rose noticed. "Now I've made you uncomfortable," she said, looking away. "I'm sorry."

"No, no, it's quite all right. I've heard of such things—I just never knew people would dare write about it."

"There are several—Gertrude Stein, Oscar Wilde, Henry James. Of course, when it comes to works about women, the poems of Sappho were likely the beginning of it all."

"Your knowledge of literature clearly exceeds mine. I know little beyond what is in Papa's collection," Ellie said. "I'm afraid I've lived a much too sheltered life. Now you've enticed me to broaden my literary horizons."

"Well, then, perhaps I've done my part for the cause today," Rose replied with a smile. "I have a book with me from an American writer I've newly discovered, Natalie Clifford Barney. You could take it with you if you'd like."

Ellie smiled back. "I'd love to, thanks." She accepted the slim volume Rose pulled from her bag. "So, what is your take on feminism?" she asked, warming to the subject.

"I think it's a very empowering idea. We are human beings with the same capacity as men to think, create, make decisions, and lead others. That's exactly why most men are so against it, in my opinion," Rose said.

"Because they don't want to lose control," she replied.

"Precisely. That's why I'm in no hurry to marry. If I was stuck with a man who told me what to do and think all the time, I believe it would crush my soul. I could never be happy with someone who didn't respect me."

"My goodness, Rose, you've just expressed what I've always felt but could never quite put into words. How exciting to have a name for it."

"It is exciting, but take my advice, Ellie. There are a great many opponents to the idea of feminism, both men and women. Be careful who's listening when you discuss it."

"I'm sure I could put my mother in that group. If she was listening to our conversation, I bet she'd faint dead away," Ellie said, giggling.

"Mine, too, but if she keeps pushing me to marry before I'm ready, I'll have to put my foot down sooner or later. You know, I don't understand why my mother is so adamant. She was pushed into a marriage that was the talk of the society pages, but she and my father can barely tolerate each other. You would think she'd want her only daughter to avoid making the same mistake."

Ellie reached out and clasped Rose's hand in a gesture of solidarity. "You won't, and neither will I."

❖

Ellie began to read her borrowed book on the way home, enthralled by the poems describing love between women. She'd read the likes of Lord Byron, Tennyson, and Shelley, yet had never been so captivated by their words of love. There was a strange but not unpleasant tension in her belly as she read, and her cheeks flushed hot as her mind conjured images to match the verses. This was not a book she could leave lying about for prying eyes to find.

Once home, she skipped in the door, energized by the afternoon's eye-opening events. She walked quickly past the parlor, hoping to avoid her mother and spend some quiet time reading in her room.

"Eleanor, is that you? Come here."

Ellie blew out a breath and hung her head. Of course she couldn't sneak by—the woman had the hearing of a bat. Tucking her book in her coat pocket, she entered the room to find her mother crocheting by the window.

"Yes, Mother?"

"Are you just now getting in? I expected you sooner."

"I told you I'd return before dinner, which isn't for another hour. Please tell me you're not springing another *unexpected* gentleman caller on me today."

"Don't be insolent. Can't a mother be glad that her children are home safe and sound?"

Ellie sighed and turned to leave, nearly colliding with the butler.

"I beg your pardon, Miss Eleanor. The mail has arrived."

"Thank you, Lyle." Ellie took the stack of envelopes from him.

"Will there be anything else, miss?"

When Ellie smiled and shook her head, he nodded and left.

"Eleanor, sort through the mail, will you? I want to finish this section."

Ellie flipped through the items. "Papa's, Papa's, oh, here's a telegram addressed to you, Mother."

"Really? Well, open it. What does it say?"

As she read the telegram, all other thoughts flew from her mind, and her heartbeat pounded in her ears. "Oh God."

"What is it?"

"It's from Aunt Evelyn. Charlie and Will were killed at the Battle of Loos, it says, two weeks ago."

Mother's shock was evident as she dropped her needlework, the blood draining from her face. "My poor sister…both boys." Her hand flew to her mouth to stifle a sob.

Ellie stood, silent, the telegram still clutched in her fingers. Images of her cousins, handsome twin boys of nineteen, raced through her mind, and she couldn't stop her tears from flowing. She remembered their holiday two summers past, before this bloody war, when she, Theo, and Mother had traveled from Surrey to Lancashire. She'd had such a wonderful time with the boys, laughing and joking as they picnicked and swam. They'd had such fun wagering chocolates on their fierce croquet matches and taking long, leisurely rides on the horses. She could picture them now, tall and fair, their blue eyes sparkling with humor and mischief. They were the pride and joy of their parents— how devastated Auntie Evelyn and Uncle Rupert must be.

Ellie's experience of the war had largely been through newspaper headlines and local gossip, until now. Now, the dead had familiar and much-loved faces. Reality had come knocking, ready to rob them all of their blissful ignorance. Her chest hurt with an ache she'd never felt before, and she pressed her fist there, silently beseeching her heart to calm.

"I should go to Evelyn," Mother said, standing abruptly. She'd allowed herself to cry for a few moments, then, ever the pragmatist, began to plan. "She'll need family with her now."

"What's the matter?"

Ellie jumped as her brother entered the room, his heels striking too heavily on the parlor floor. "We've had a telegram, Theo. The boys...they're dead." Her throat constricted as if squeezed by an invisible hand, and no more words would come.

"The boys," Theo repeated. He took the telegram from her hand and read it. "Christ."

"Theodore Winthrop, mind your tongue," their mother said automatically.

Ellie's brother was a strapping lad of seventeen and, while generally easygoing, was fully possessed of their mother's temper when provoked. "Sorry, but for both of them to die— bloody Huns." His face grew ruddy as he clenched the slip of paper in his fist. "Come December I'll be eighteen. Then I can join up and fight the devils."

Mother gasped. "You'll do no such thing. I'll not lose my son, too."

Theo thankfully knew when to shut his mouth. Ellie looked at his baby face and unruly red-blond hair. *He may be tall, but he's just a boy.* The thought of him marching off to war made her stomach sick.

She needed to move, to do something. She walked over to the newfangled telephone on its stand. Mother still regarded it as a passing fad. "Should I ring Papa at the office?"

"No, Eleanor, you needn't bother him. We'll talk later. Now, I've got to make preparations. I think taking the train from London would be best."

"I'll go with you, Mother," she said. "I'm sure Anna will need some support as well."

"Oh, dear, poor Anna. I'd forgotten. And to think she and Charlie had planned to be married in the spring."

Ellie had known Anna for some years now and loved her like the younger sister she'd never had. She wanted to comfort her in her grief, but—she thought with a twinge of guilt—having an excuse to leave and avoid the hopeful suitors who had somehow found her interesting this past London season sounded like a blessed reprieve.

"She'll certainly need her friends beside her."

"Very well." Mother could hardly argue with Ellie's reasoning. "I'll be glad for your company on the trip. Theodore, ring for Jones and have her meet me in my dressing room. I must begin packing."

A few moments later, the lady's maid arrived and Ellie approached her. "Yes, miss?"

"Lady Violet needs you upstairs in her dressing room, Jones," she told her. "We'll be packing for a trip."

"Yes, miss." The girl wasn't much older than Ellie herself, but she looked weary at the prospect.

"I imagine she'll only be taking her black dresses—that should pare it down for you," Ellie said, managing a smile. Jones nodded and hurried away.

Ellie joined her brother at the window overlooking the colorless, pruned-back west gardens, their soggy drabness matching her deteriorating mood. They were silent for several minutes.

Then he said, "At least half the boys in upper sixth form are going to join the fight. It's all anyone talks about at school. I want to join the cavalry so I can ride and work with the horses. We've all got to do our bit, haven't we?"

"Mother and Papa are never going to allow you to enlist, Theo."

"I'll be eighteen and a man, and I'll do as I please," Theo responded. "Besides, Papa will support me. He fought in the Boer War and knows it's a man's duty to defend his country. Even Jimmy down at the stables gave Papa his notice this morning."

"Oh no. Theo, haven't you read the papers? This war that was supposed to be buttoned up in six months has only gotten worse. The casualties are quite high." She noticed he blanched a little at that, but then he lifted his chin.

"All the more reason for us to band together and overpower the enemy. You won't change my mind, Ellie."

She looked at her little brother, now taller than she was, and felt a profound sense of foreboding. With tears in her eyes, she laid a hand on his arm. "I suppose I won't, but I shan't be happy to see you go off to war. It would devastate us all if something happened to you."

Theo just looked away, and they stood in silence, gazing out at their corner of the world and wondering what would become of it.

❖

Johanna Lennox boarded the train and found an empty seat, stowing her case on the floor. It was the last leg of her long journey from Edinburgh to Boulogne-sur-Mer, and she was tired. Maybe she could get a wee bit of rest…

"Oh, hello."

Johanna blinked at the young woman who had just taken the seat across from her, looking so cheerful she thought she might burst. Johanna could tell she was a new recruit, dressed up in her chambray blue uniform with perfectly starched white apron and cap, and hadn't seen a speck of this horrible war in person. She nodded and averted her eyes, not in the mood for idle chit-chat, but she feared that wouldn't stop the lass from trying.

"Excuse me, Sister." Johanna sighed inwardly, her fears affirmed. "Are you headed to the coast? It would be ever so funny if we were going to the same place, don't you think? This'll be my first posting, mind—I've come straight from training, but I'm ever so excited to care for our brave Tommies at the front. I'm Fannie Gibson, by the way."

Johanna looked at the outstretched hand before her, then up at the girl's sweet, oblivious smile. Summoning a fair bit more human decency than she felt at the moment, she shook Fannie's hand. "Johanna Lennox."

"It's ever so lovely to meet you, Miss Lennox. The other girls and I," Fannie said, nodding toward the adjacent seat's occupants, "we're VADs."

The chipper little thing seemed so proud that Johanna managed not to roll her eyes. The Voluntary Aid Detachments had exploded with legions of eager young women looking to find a bit of excitement in the war zone, but she'd yet to determine if they were of a tough enough constitution to do the work they were headed for. Johanna nodded and looked out the window at the deceptively idyllic countryside passing by. After two years of training in Edinburgh and London, she was headed to a base hospital on the northern coast of France. Her patients at home had been weeks or months removed from the battlefield, but their wounded bodies and minds told the story of what they had been forced to endure. She was impatient to be of greater service to the men out there in the thick of it.

"We're going to be setting up a canteen at the station, they told us. We'll serve soup and cocoa and…Oh, look! Aren't they handsome?"

The chatterbox's face was pressed to the window. They were slowing down as they approached the rail station, and Fannie had caught sight of a detachment of British soldiers marching by. Johanna took a closer look at the men that had Fannie all atwitter. They looked grim and worn out to her.

"Just in from the front, I reckon," she remarked.

"Oh, the poor dears," Fannie moaned, her hands clasped to her bosom in overly dramatic fashion.

Johanna sighed, feeling a great deal older than her twenty-four years. "We are in a damned bloody war, you know. I hope you don't expect things to be all waving flags and fancy parades."

Fannie looked at her, shocked. Perhaps the coarse language had offended her. Johanna stifled a smile, hoping she had knocked a bit of innocence off the lass. She'd need a much thicker skin if she was to survive here. Johanna sighed again and looked away, noticing her own reflection in the window— her dark hair was a bit mussed, and frown lines creased her pale face. *Go easy, Lennox—no need to be such a bloody cynic.*

"Well, of course…Mummy told me it would be difficult, that I mightn't like it one bit," Fannie said. She lowered her voice and said in a loud whisper, "I've seen men with missing arms and legs, you know. We got quite used to it in training."

"And what made you decide to join the VADs?" Johanna didn't really want to prolong this conversation, but she had a sneaking suspicion.

"Oh, for the adventure," Fannie replied, confirming her guess. "Nothing exciting ever happens at home, and all the boys have gone off." Seeming to remember herself, she sobered. "But mostly, I joined up to offer my services to my country and its brave fighting men."

This time Johanna couldn't help but roll her eyes. "Och, lass, we'll see what you're made of soon enough."

## CHAPTER TWO

As the train rumbled north, Ellie was struck by how much things had changed since the last time she'd traveled. She'd been younger then, of course, but so fancy-free, so happy about going on holiday. The hustle and bustle of people, the sounds and smells of the big city had been so exciting. Her memories were vivid, colorful, and so very different from what she saw before her now.

She'd been particularly focused on people today and hadn't seen a single smile, even on the faces of children. Everyone seemed so serious, so careworn, and Ellie wondered how many had experienced what her aunt and uncle were now facing. A great many, she imagined, glancing down at the copy of *The Times* she'd purchased in London. Today's published casualty list had filled two full pages. Looking out the window, she could at least see splotches of color in the passing autumn countryside, reds and yellows improving the dreary palette of gray, brown, and so much black surrounding her.

Mother stirred in her seat across from Ellie and opened her eyes. "Dear me, I must've dozed off. Where are we?"

"Nearly there, I think. Who's meeting us?"

"Rupert is sending the car," Mother replied.

Ellie's breath hitched as a pang of anxiety stabbed her chest. "I've no idea what to say," she said, her eyes burning with tears. "How can we possibly ease their pain?"

"We'll provide whatever is needed, even if that means just sitting with them in silence. I learned that when your Grandmama passed. Knowing that others share your grief sometimes helps. I do admire you for wanting to come, Eleanor. I'm afraid it won't be a very pleasant visit."

"I know, but I couldn't just sit at home thinking about it. One cannot help those in need if one is not willing to experience some discomfort," she said.

Mother looked at her strangely.

"What is it?" Ellie asked.

"That was a very wise thing to say, Eleanor. Just so—we'll support them however we can." She reached out and gave Ellie's hand an awkward pat. "The loss of Charlie and Will has reminded me that we mustn't take our loved ones for granted. Thank you for coming with me."

Ellie caught her hand and gave it a gentle squeeze, touched at this rare expression of affection from her undemonstrative mother. "You're welcome."

❖

The black band of mourning stood out in sharp relief on the chauffeur's white sleeve as he opened the car door. "Phillips, isn't it?" Ellie asked, accepting his hand.

"Yes, miss."

"How have things been for you all, Phillips?"

The old chauffeur looked at her in surprise. "I shouldn't like to speak out of turn, miss, but it's been a terrible shock. The young masters were so full of life, they were."

"Yes, indeed. I imagine it's been difficult for everyone. Do let me know if I can help, won't you?"

Phillips's eyes widened, but he touched his cap with a nod. "Thank you, miss."

Mother gave Ellie the familiar look of reproach she used when she'd committed some real or imagined breach of etiquette. "Why must you carry on such overly familiar conversations with the staff?" she whispered. "It's unseemly."

Ellie sighed. "That was hardly a conversation, Mother, and why should it be unseemly to offer sympathy to another person? Phillips and most of the others have known the boys since they were babies. I'm sure some sense of grief has traveled downstairs."

Mother sniffed. "Still," she said. "You know I'm just trying to raise you to be a respectable young lady."

"I am well-educated, well-read, and well-dressed. I have never kissed a boy, and I eat my soup with the correct spoon. I'm fairly certain that qualifies me as respectable."

Mother just huffed and looked out the window. She didn't speak again on the drive, and Ellie tamped down her irritation at her old-fashioned ways. Mother had been raised to observe a very strict delineation between the social classes, something Ellie often chafed against, to her mother's great embarrassment. She was not unkind, exactly, but she expected people to know their places and stay there. There was no point in arguing—Ellie didn't expect her to change.

Black armbands were present on all four of the staff who met their arrival. Ellie looked at the manor, its gray stone bearing dark streaks from a recent rain, and fancied that even the house seemed melancholy. As the footman helped them out of the car, Aunt Evelyn emerged from her home. She was dressed all in black and looked as if she hadn't slept in days.

"Oh, Evelyn," Mother said, clasping both her hands and kissing her cheek.

"It's good of you to come, Violet," Aunt Evelyn said quietly. "And Ellie, it's lovely to see you, my dear."

"Aunt Evelyn," she managed, as her eyes again filled with tears. Any words she'd planned to say seemed so trivial now, in the face of such grief. Aunt Evelyn nodded and patted her cheek, then turned and walked back inside.

❖

After a quiet supper, they all gathered in the parlor, and the grief in the room was almost tangible. Uncle Rupert sat by the fireplace, gazing into the flames, his pipe unlit in his hand, as if he had forgotten what to do with it. Aunt Evelyn sat in her armchair by the window, perfectly still except for the rise and fall of her shoulders when she sighed. Ellie's mother puttered about, picking imaginary lint off the chair cushions and straightening things that didn't need to be straightened.

Ellie watched all of this with a deep sense of despair. She hated that she couldn't do or say a thing that would really help, and witnessing her aunt's and uncle's pain was the worst thing she'd ever experienced. Sitting still, powerless, was driving her mad.

"Aunt Evelyn, would you like some tea?" she said. When there was no answer, she tried again. "Auntie?"

Aunt Evelyn started and looked around, blinking until her eyes focused on Ellie. "What? I'm sorry, dear, did you say something?"

"Yes, Auntie. I was wondering if you might like some tea."

"Oh, that's sweet of you, Ellie. Yes, some chamomile would be lovely. Forgive me, dear—my mind was elsewhere just now."

"I'll ring for it," Mother said, no doubt happy for something to do.

Ellie nodded and took her aunt's hand. "You seemed very far away, Auntie. Are you all right?"

Aunt Evelyn shrugged. "I don't know if I'll ever be all right again, but we must carry on, mustn't we?"

Ellie squeezed her hand, not knowing what to say. Her mother came back from speaking to the maid and sat with them in silence. The tea arrived in short order, and Ellie poured them all a cup. Aunt Evelyn took a sip or two, then set her cup down hard, a sob escaping her throat.

"Reverend Williams came by yesterday about a service for the boys," she said, her voice shaking, "but I don't know if I can manage it. They've buried my babies in some godforsaken place, and we don't even know where. This awful war took their lives, and now they can't even rest on home soil. How can their souls ever find peace in a place of such violence and misery?"

As tears streamed down Ellie's face, she heard a strangled cry. Uncle Rupert stood and flung his pipe away, looking wild-eyed at his wife. "Don't you say such things, Evie. Our sons are in heaven, and their souls are free. It has to be so. I can't bear to think of anything else." He stood, trembling, then lurched out of the room.

"Oh God," Aunt Evelyn said, and she ran after her husband.

Ellie looked at her mother, shocked at what she'd just heard. "Is it true, Mother? Our dead soldiers aren't sent home to their families, but just buried where they've fallen?" She'd been quite young when her grandmother died, but she knew there had been graveside services. The family had at least been able to say their good-byes.

Mother sniffed. "Yes, it's true, and it's all just too much to contemplate. Try not to think of it, Eleanor." She stood then, her face tearstained and weary. "I'm going to bed."

Ellie sat there for a long time after, reflecting on the reality of war. In her ignorance, she hadn't thought about the logistical impossibility of sending such vast numbers of casualties home for burial. Her thoughts turned to Charlie and Will, their bright lights snuffed out, and their parents unable even to lay flowers upon their graves. Her chest ached with the sheer unfairness of it all.

Ellie sent word to the Browning residence the next morning, informing Anna that she was up from Surrey. Now, on the third day of her trip, she had come together with her friend for a much-needed visit. Anna's black and white spaniel ran ahead as she and Ellie strolled arm in arm around the grounds of the manor house. The air was cool but the sunshine warm, releasing the heady fragrance of ripe fruit from the orchards. A nearby farmer's sheep were little white puffs against the distant hills, and Uncle Rupert's horses grazed contentedly in the pasture.

"I think Mother Nature gave us such a glorious day to lighten our moods. Is it wrong of me to enjoy it?" Ellie said.

"Not at all. Perhaps the lesson is never to take a single thing for granted. Thank you for this, Ellie," Anna said, squeezing her arm. "I simply couldn't bear any more sympathetic looks, and if one more person asks me how I'm feeling, I may scream."

Ellie completely understood. In recent days she'd witnessed how people's well-meaning reactions to grief could be stifling. "I think you're doing quite well, considering. Your strength is remarkable." Anna and Charlie had been childhood sweethearts and very much in love. Ellie doubted she would be as resilient in her shoes.

"Thank you. I don't feel very strong sometimes—I've cried enough for a lifetime, believe me. But Charlie was always so cheerful, it seems wrong of me to languish in my sadness. I feel as if I must enjoy life for the both of us." She wiped away a tear and smiled.

Ellie put an arm around Anna's shoulders. "What do you say we go into the village today? I'm sure we could find something to occupy ourselves for a while."

Anna brightened. "What a splendid idea—do you think your uncle would let us take the car? I've learned to drive, you know."

"You haven't," Ellie exclaimed, envious. "Your father allowed it?"

"He gave in to my incessant badgering, more like. I can be very persuasive when I want something."

"Will you teach me?" Ellie asked. The idea of coming and going as she pleased was thrilling.

"Of course. Mother and I came in the carriage today— she thinks motor cars are terrifying. But I could pick you up tomorrow for a lesson."

Ellie felt giddy with excitement. "Let's not ask Uncle Rupert today, then. We'll go off on our own adventure tomorrow."

The next morning, much to her mother's disapproval, Ellie hopped into Anna's two-seater Ford and they set off for the village. It was another beautiful day, with only a few clouds scudding across the sky. The views of the moors were magnificent, and Ellie felt lighter than she had in quite some time. As they entered the village, she took in the sights. A half dozen rowdy schoolboys were kicking a makeshift football in the street, dodging traffic and the cuffs of irritated adults. Some folks walked about, shopping or doing the day's business, but a growing crowd of women had clustered near the post office.

"What do you think is happening there?" she asked Anna.

"I thought it was maybe a suffragist gathering, but that hasn't been happening much since the war began," Anna replied, pulling off to the side of the street.

"Have you attended any of those?" Though Ellie discussed the cause of women's suffrage with her friends and read about it in the papers, she hadn't heard any speeches in person.

"Oh yes," Anna said. "I heard Emmeline Pankhurst speak in Manchester before the war."

"A friend of mine mentioned that just this week. How was it?"

"It was all very dramatic, what with people shouting and cheering. Imagine having the right to vote! Of course, the male establishment is fighting back, but still, it's exciting to think about what could happen in the future."

Ellie thought about what Rose Talbot had said. "The war has made me believe that anything is possible. Look at all those women stepping right in to take over the men's jobs. It's quite inspiring, don't you think?"

Anna turned to Ellie suddenly and grasped her hand. "Don't you wish there was something we could do, too? With Charlie gone, I can't stand the thought of just sitting around while more and more of our soldiers die. But I can't very well march off to the factories—my father would disown me."

"I know what you mean, but we've never had a job before. Who would want us?" A cheer rose up from the group of women on the street, and Ellie's curiosity overcame her. "Let's go see what they're so happy about."

As they neared the crowd, one voice rose above the rest. Ellie caught a glimpse of a woman in a blue and white uniform standing on an overturned crate. "Help is urgently needed, ladies," she intoned. "The Red Cross is in dire need of strong, courageous women to volunteer as cooks, cleaning maids, clerks, drivers, and of course, nursing members. This is the ultimate act of charity we can offer for Britain and her soldiers. I urge you to sign up today."

Excited chatter erupted around them as Ellie looked at Anna. Then Anna, wide-eyed, nodded and, with a resolute smile, pulled her forward. Ellie knew what she was thinking and her pulse quickened—they had just heard a call they were compelled to answer.

## CHAPTER THREE

"Y ou did *what?*"
Ellie could tell Mother was beside herself—her face looked strained, as if her corset was much too tight. She added this to the long list of ways she'd disappointed her mother, who had hoped, in vain, for a demure and compliant daughter.

"Mother, this is a wonderful opportunity to help. Thousands of women are signing up with the Voluntary Aid Detachments." Her stomach was in knots, but she held her voice steady.

"Thousands of crazy women, you mean. Why in the world would you want to go to a foreign country, during a war, and be exposed to God knows what?" Mother began to pace the sitting room. "And how will you ever land a suitable husband if you're flitting about overseas, *cleaning?*"

"I will be training for basic nursing care, not working as a scullery maid. And besides, Mother, if we don't help out where we can, there won't be any men left to marry." Ellie didn't say that getting married was far from her goal in life—she had to spare her poor mother any more stress at the moment.

"Well, that's just ridiculous," Mother sputtered. "The war is bound to be over soon."

"That's what we thought a year ago, and many tens of thousands have died since." Deciding to try a different tack, Ellie softened her voice and took her mother's hands. "Anna is going, Mother. I feel strongly that she shouldn't go alone, not after the shock she's suffered. I can look after her and still do my part for king and country."

"Let her go, Violet." Aunt Evelyn spoke quietly from the doorway.

Mother spun around. "Surely you don't agree with this foolishness, Evelyn."

Aunt Evelyn crossed the room and stopped to gaze out a window. "I spent nearly two decades taking care of my boys, doing my best to keep them safe. From the moment they went off to war, I felt utterly useless. I could no longer do a bloody thing to help them," she said, her voice breaking. "If I were young, I'd join up right beside Ellie and be happy to do it. Your daughter is a courageous and compassionate young woman, dear sister. Let her forge her own path in this life while she can."

Mother had been effectively shocked into silence. Ellie went to Aunt Evelyn with tears in her eyes. "Thank you, Auntie, for understanding."

Aunt Evelyn turned and gathered Ellie into her arms, her embrace strengthened by her conviction. "Go, my dear. Go and do for those boys what I couldn't do for my own."

❖

Ellie and Anna were giddy over what they had done. Neither of them had ever asserted themselves so boldly, and it felt exhilarating. Mother had telephoned Ellie's father and tried desperately to sway him to her side of the argument, but he had surprised both of them by supporting Ellie's decision. Now there was nothing left to do but go forward with their plan.

Although they initially had intended to stay together, Anna ended up signing on to become an ambulance driver, while Ellie wanted to work in nursing.

"Your names will be sent off to London in the morning," the recruiter said, as Ellie and Anna put their signatures to paper. "Please follow this list regarding what to pack, and be prepared to depart for training in two days' time. Miss Winthrop, you shall have a probationary period of one month at a city hospital before you will be allowed to sign on officially for foreign service, if you so choose. Miss Browning, you shall report to Red Cross headquarters in London. Thank you in advance, ladies, for your service."

The recruiter handed them each a letter from Katherine Furse, the leader of the Voluntary Aid Detachment movement, thanking them for their service, and reminding them how much their country needed them. Now that she'd decided, Ellie felt a burst of patriotism and pride, and she couldn't wait to leave.

"What do you think it'll be like in France?" Anna asked, as they took a walk on their last afternoon together.

"Pretty grim, I imagine. Our barrister's son was wounded in Belgium in one of our army's first battles, and he said it all seemed like a fatal exercise in futility."

Anna blanched, no doubt thinking of her beloved Charlie. "Have you ever wondered if there could have been another solution, instead of generals ordering their men to slaughter one another? What will anyone have gained when it's all over? Will their deaths have any meaning?"

Ellie's chest hurt as she watched the tears track down Anna's cheeks. "I don't know if there's any reason that could ever be worth such a loss of life, but ultimately, all we can do is support the poor souls following those generals' orders, and with any luck, we'll be able to save a few."

"With any luck, my friend," Anna said, wiping her tears and straightening her shoulders with the strength and resolve Ellie had come to admire. "With any luck."

# CHAPTER FOUR

*Five weeks later*

A path led from the hospital compound down a small slope to the sea, and from there, Johanna could see the great white hospital ships in the distance as they carried the lucky ones back to Britain. She felt blessed to be stationed here, for the sea soothed her—had since she was a child in her mam's arms watching her da bring in the day's catch. She needed these rare moments when she could just stand here and breathe, to let the salty breeze cleanse her mind.

Her baptism into wartime nursing had been swift and harsh. Never had she seen wounds like these, so violent and raw. Surrounded by horror and pain and fear, the feeling of despair never loosened its grip. Johanna was exhausted and heartsore, sustained only by the knowledge that she was doing some small bit of good in this horrible place.

It had been a long and demanding shift and she needed to rest, but she lingered, watching the waves. Johanna's relationship with the sea was complex. She'd loved it growing up, when she'd chase the gulls, dig for clams in the surf, and explore the open water on Da's boat, listening to his stories and looking for selkie folk. Then she'd hated the angry sea that took her da and brother one awful stormy afternoon. Now, existing as she was in a constant state of stress and crisis, she needed the sights and sounds of the sea to preserve her sanity.

"Ambulances coming! Ambulances coming!"

Johanna closed her eyes, wanting to escape for a bit longer, but it was no use. Duty had beckoned, and with a sigh, she turned to answer its call.

She had just finished serving morning tea to the men in the surgical ward when the hospital matron found her.

"A new group of volunteers is coming in tomorrow, Sister Lennox," Matron said. "I'd like you to meet them at the station and accompany them back here."

"But Matron Campbell, the last lot were more trouble than they were worth. Why have we got to take on these hoity-toity society types who have never known a moment of hard work?"

"Now, be fair, Lennox. A few haven't been up to snuff, but most have pulled their weight quite well. Tell me you'd rather be washing bandages and mopping floors instead of them."

She had a point. The VADs had given them more time to focus on the patients, where they were desperately needed. Still, they came here, barely trained, with grand ideas of being nurses, when the professional nurses had worked for years to earn the title of Sister. It was beyond irritating. Matron Campbell, a fellow Scot, tolerated Johanna's irascible feelings on the subject, but at the end of the day, her word ruled.

"I've decided to put you in charge of this group and their training," Matron went on.

"Och, you haven't done!" Johanna was quickly silenced by The Look, the one that made the younger girls nearly wet themselves. Matron was a kind and decent woman, but she could be very imposing when she had to be.

"You are one of my best nurses, Lennox, and I want these volunteers brought up to speed quickly. I have great faith in your ability to do just that."

"Humph." There was no point in arguing, so Johanna just grumbled and nodded.

"That's a good lass. There's a transport leaving in the morning that'll take you to the station to meet the train."

"How many are coming?" Johanna asked, trying to prepare herself mentally for the task.

"I was told five—three nursing volunteers, a cook, and a laundress. You'll primarily work with the nursing VADs, showing them the different wards and the duties within each, as well as the general rules of behavior. I'll expect weekly reports on their progress and capabilities. Now, I must join Dr. Samuel for rounds. Have you any questions, Sister?"

Johanna sighed. "Nae, Matron." The older woman looked at her for a moment, gave a small smile and a wink, and left her to her work.

❖

By the next morning, Johanna couldn't help but feel a bit of excitement, despite the reason for her excursion. A driver took her, along with six soldiers deemed fit to return to their units, to Boulogne, and dropped them at the entrance to the rail station building. She bid the soldiers farewell and good luck, then turned to the driver.

"I've got some supplies to pick up, Sister, but I can meet you here when I've finished. Your new arrivals should be here by then."

"Thank you, Private." The young man touched his cap and drove off.

Johanna stood on the worn wooden platform and took in her surroundings. She hadn't been away from the hospital for weeks, and she felt exhilarated by the different kind of chaos outside of its confines. Motorized vehicles and horse-drawn conveyances vied for space on the street, and old women in black shawls peddled apples and flowers to passersby. The busy hum of a hundred voices was a welcome change from the moans and shouts of men in pain. Just beyond the platform, a sergeant barked orders to a group of soldiers, new arrivals by the look of their pressed khakis and clean puttees. She felt a pang of worry for the fresh-faced lads and contemplated the likelihood that some would end up in their wards at the base hospital.

A distant whistle told of the train's impending arrival, and Johanna's thoughts reluctantly turned to her task. Was Matron off her head, putting her in charge of the volunteers? She was no teacher—she had little patience and even less tolerance for frivolity and nonsense. She was here to do her job and didn't need any interference. Still, Matron Campbell had been good to her, and out of respect for her fellow Scotswoman, she'd have to try her best.

She watched as the train rumbled to a stop, the great black engine belching blacker smoke. In only a few moments, the platform was swarming with people as the passengers disembarked. She searched the crowd until, toward the far end, she caught sight of four heads clad in the white handkerchief caps of the VADs. The women stood still for a bit, looking around, until one seemed to take charge. She strode briskly in Johanna's direction, and the others followed in her wake like little blue and white ducklings. The leader was rather tall, like Johanna, and reddish-blond curls escaped from her cap. As Johanna stepped forward to intercept them, she turned startling blue eyes to her and smiled. Johanna almost smiled back, the woman's confidence and open, friendly face taking her by surprise. Remembering her role and wanting to establish her authority, Johanna schooled her features and spoke sternly.

"Ladies, I am Sister Lennox, and I will be taking you to the hospital to which you've been assigned. I was told to expect five—where is the other volunteer?"

Blue Eyes spoke right up, still smiling. "Miss Andrews has taken ill and couldn't come. It's just the four of us." The others nodded, wide-eyed.

"Humph." Johanna checked her list and called the names. The last name, Miss Eleanor Winthrop, belonged to Blue Eyes, and she nodded. "Come along then—the transport should be waiting." Before Johanna turned to walk away, she noticed Miss Winthrop's smile falter as she exchanged glances with the others. Johanna felt a bit guilty for her brusque manner...but only a wee bit.

❖

The moment Ellie laid eyes on the nurse who had come to meet them, her nervousness grew. Sister Lennox gave quite a powerful first impression. Tall, confident, and strikingly beautiful, she immediately commanded attention, like an actress on the London stage. Yet the warm welcome Ellie had hoped for was absent. Under the intense appraisal of those slate gray eyes, she suddenly felt she would be found sorely lacking, and her stomach twisted with apprehension.

When Sister Lennox barked for them to follow, Ellie glanced at the other girls and knew they felt as she did. With a spark of determination, she shrugged and fell in behind the quickly retreating nurse. Surely the rest of the hospital staff would be glad of their arrival. She would not let one prickly nurse get the best of her.

They stepped into the busy street beside a canvas-covered transport lorry. They were handed up into the back by the driver and sat on hard wooden benches across from each other, clutching their bags. Sister Lennox sat up front with the driver, and as they got underway, the noise of the engine afforded them the chance to talk without being overheard.

"Golly gosh, she's a tad unfriendly," Daisy Chamberlain said, her round cheeks pink with indignation.

"There were a couple like that at the convalescent home where I trained," Mary Ingram replied. "Seems the regular nurses get a bit tetchy about the volunteers, as if we're after their jobs or some such poppycock."

"Well, she could have been more welcoming is all I'm saying," Daisy said.

Thankful that the third girl, Margaret Ross, didn't seem inclined to chime in, Ellie spoke up. "I imagine Sister Lennox is under a great deal of strain, but whatever the reason, I shall endeavor to stay on her good side. We'll just do our part to represent VADs in the best possible light, right, girls?"

The others murmured their agreement. They bounced along the rutted dirt roads to their destination, unable to see much through the flapping canvas over the tailgate. Ellie's backside was quite tender by the time they arrived, but no matter, they were finally here. They stepped out of the vehicle to see rows and rows of long white buildings, and planks over the muddy ground made pathways between them. Nurses and orderlies rushed to and fro, and a group of convalescing soldiers whistled as the newcomers got their first look at General Hospital No. 7.

"Look, they're VADs," one said. "Very Adorable Darlings, that's what they call 'em. Hallo, ladies, I'm Tommy." Then he grinned and swatted the shoulder of the man beside him. "But then, we're all Tommies, eh, lads?" The soldier, who barely looked old enough to shave, thought he was very amusing as his comrades guffawed and slapped each other's backs.

It was good-natured joking, but Ellie felt her cheeks flame. Margaret likewise looked uncomfortable, but Daisy and Mary smiled and waved coquettishly. Ellie jumped at a loud voice beside her.

"Ladies, you will come with me now." Sister Lennox leveled a glare at the men, and Tommy ducked his head sheepishly.

"Sorry, Sister," he called.

Ellie and the others followed her past several buildings to a cluster of small timber and canvas huts. Sister Lennox opened the door of one and motioned them inside. "These are your sleeping quarters. Choose a bed and leave your bag beneath it for now."

Ellie looked at the thin mattresses on their metal frames, upon each of which sat a stack of white utilitarian linens. She chose the cot closest to the door and stowed her belongings. She'd barely straightened up when Sister Lennox barked another command.

"Look smart, ladies. You will now report to the matron."

Ellie smoothed her skirt and tucked a loose strand of hair beneath her cap, then followed Sister Lennox, hoping the matron was a little less formidable.

## CHAPTER FIVE

It's a pleasure to meet you, ladies, and we're glad you're here." Matron Campbell's greeting was kind and welcoming, and Ellie took a deep breath, trying to calm her nerves.

"I'm sure you learned in your training that there is important and difficult work ahead. Miss Ross, you will be introduced to our chief laundress shortly. As for you nursing volunteers, Sister Lennox will be directly supervising your group."

Ellie nearly groaned aloud and could swear a smirk raced across Matron's face. Their new taskmaster stood, stoic and unmoving, as Matron listed the rules of conduct, which covered requirements of punctuality, adherence to protocol, and avoidance of overly familiar behavior with soldiers or staff.

"Are there any questions about these rules?"

"No, ma'am," they said.

"Let me be very clear. I run a tight ship, not to be harsh, but because it is necessary to keep the hospital running smoothly. I need you at your best—therefore, you will learn from the best." She gestured toward Sister Lennox, who had the grace to nod in acknowledgment of the praise. "Now, I'll let you get to it, but there's one more thing—I strongly suggest that you cut your hair shorter and keep it tucked up under your caps, due to the infestations of lice that arrive on the men."

Ellie felt a little ill at the thought, and the other girls gasped in dismay.

"I'll not sugarcoat this for you, ladies. You will see and do things here that you've scarcely imagined, for which your training could not prepare you. You will live and work in conditions that you've likely never experienced. But the care of our brave men must rise above these discomforts. It is why you are here."

Ellie glanced at Sister Lennox then and swore she saw the glint of challenge in her eye. She expected them to crumble, to fail, and Ellie felt a fierce resolve to prove her wrong. She would get no such satisfaction out of Eleanor Winthrop.

Their first afternoon at the hospital entailed an introduction to the nursing staff and orderlies, a quick demonstration of their various tasks, and a thorough tour of the wards. This last brought crystal clear awareness to Ellie's reality and purpose. The smells assaulted her first—the sharp tang of blood, the awful stink of trench foot and gangrene, the strong tar-like odor of carbolic soap. Then she focused her gaze on the patients, in various states of trauma, from simple fractures to missing limbs and ruined faces. Ellie swallowed hard, fighting back tears at the horror of it. These men, shattered in body and mind, needed them.

"Your efficient work will help maintain order," Sister Lennox said, brisk and direct as she laid out her expectations. "You have arrived on an unusually quiet day, but chaos can erupt quickly when the wounded come in. You are expected to provide a clean and well-stocked environment so that the doctors and nursing sisters can care for the men. Is that understood?"

"Yes, Sister."

By the time she fell onto her cot that evening, Ellie had made up thirty beds with clean linens and carted the soiled linens to the laundry area, where Margaret was already hard at work, boiling soiled uniforms in a huge steaming vat. She'd swept Ward A twice, rolled and stacked several dozen bandages, and helped serve tea to a hundred men. Her feet burned and her back ached, but she felt a satisfying sense of accomplishment—she was needed and truly useful, perhaps for the first time in her life.

Ellie fell into a steady rhythm by the end of that week and thought she was doing quite well, certainly better than Daisy, who fumbled about, sighing and moaning about her sore feet. Ellie wanted to slap the self-centered little twit—could she not see the far greater suffering around her? And yet the patients, broken and riddled with pain as they were, spoke to the volunteers with great respect and gratitude for the least bit of comfort they provided.

Sister Lennox noticed, for Ellie had heard her speaking sternly to Daisy more than once. Ellie frequently felt her eyes on her, too, watching her work, appraising her efforts, but they'd had little conversation beyond the perfunctory *good morning* or simple directives. Ellie was surprised, then, when Matron sent for her in her third week for a discussion in her office.

"Miss Winthrop, how are you getting on?" she asked.

"Fairly well, I think, Matron," she replied, suddenly nervous. *What if I'm not doing well at all?*

"Hmm, yes, well…Sister Lennox has spoken to me about you."

The tiny butterflies in Ellie's stomach exploded into a flock of starlings, wheeling and diving as she stared at Matron's shoes.

"Miss Winthrop."

Ellie raised her eyes to find Matron smiling at her. "She says you have exceeded expectations and done an excellent job thus far. I'm told you have even picked up the slack of other less…efficient volunteers. Well done."

"Thank you, Matron Campbell," Ellie said, and the starlings flew away.

"Sister Lennox also says that you have an exceptionally calm and compassionate demeanor with the patients. Therefore, I would like to increase your direct care duties. Three more volunteers are expected later this week, which will free you to assist the sisters in Wards A and B."

Ellie was fit to burst with excitement, but she tried to keep her voice calm. "I'm grateful for the opportunity, Matron. Thank you."

"No, thank *you*, Miss Winthrop. You will soon begin accompanying Sister Lennox on her rounds. She will let you know when. Now, I'd best let you get back to your duties. Good day to you." Matron dismissed her with a smile.

Ellie could feel her cheeks flush with pride as she walked back to the ward with a new spring in her step. Sister Lennox, the gruff and critical Scotswoman, liked her work and had commended her to the matron. Ellie had no idea why her opinion mattered so much, but she felt as if she'd just won a prize.

❖

Johanna noticed quickly that Blue Eyes had a way about her. The wounded had been coming in thick and fast, and they could barely keep up some days, yet Winthrop never failed to offer encouragement and comfort with a word, a touch. She showed no outward distress, no matter the condition of the patient. Johanna had seen Winthrop helping Sister Claire tend to a young man who had lost both legs and part of an arm. The changing of his dressings was agony for him, but she'd laid a gentle hand on his brow, distracting him with talk of home as she calmly massaged his remaining limb. The men had begun to ask for her—*Sister Sunshine*, they called, *where is Sister Sunshine?* Though Winthrop had not earned the title of Sister, Johanna didn't correct them, for Winthrop had become every bit as important to their care as any of the nurses.

The leadership Johanna observed on that first day at the station had been of immense help to her. Winthrop, with far more patience than Johanna possessed, directed and instructed the other VADs, but she did so in such a kind manner, they rarely minded. Johanna hated to admit it, but she'd been wrong about the usefulness of these volunteers. They were, for the most part, a good lot, but the star of the group, hands down, was Eleanor Winthrop.

"Sister Lennox?" The pleasant voice of her daydream jolted her back to the moment. Winthrop stood before her, face flushed and hands wringing in agitation.

"What is it, Winthrop?"

"The new girl, Miss Adams, has frozen stock still, refusing to assist with bathing. Apparently the thought of seeing a naked man is too much for her to bear. She just keeps saying *I couldn't, oh, I couldn't!* She won't listen to me, and I hate to bother Matron, but we've got a truckload of filthy soldiers to clean up and no time for such balderdash. Do come and talk sense into her, won't you?"

Johanna had to stifle a smile at the flitting hands and righteous indignation of this usually imperturbable woman. Her pink cheeks and flashing blue eyes reminded Johanna, not for the first time, what a bright spot she was in this dreary place. Tamping down her mirth, Johanna agreed to come straightaway and was rewarded with a smile that enchanted her like a firefly in the darkness. She realized with some surprise that the patients weren't the only ones enjoying their moments with Sister Sunshine.

## CHAPTER SIX

*Late December, 1915*

Ellie had gotten precious little sleep due to the bitter cold and ineradicable vermin that plagued them all, but nevertheless, the call came to get to the wards. By the time she arrived, the place was swarming with wounded. There was the usual destruction caused by shrapnel and bullets, shock and trench foot, but she noticed a new symptom in many of the patients. Tears streamed down dirty faces and hands clawed at throats as the men gasped for air or vomited a frothy yellow substance.

"What is it?" she asked a passing sister.

"Poison gas," the nurse said, her voice trembling. "Just drifted in on the wind, they say." Her eyes filled with tears. "Did they not have enough ways to suffer?"

Ellie thought she could no longer be shocked by anything in this damnable place. She set about removing clothing and boots, stiff with blood and stinking mud. They washed the men as best they could, changing water three or four times per man while removing weeks of grime and sweat. This simple act gave such dignity and pleasure to the men, despite their pain and distress.

"Miss Winthrop, over here." Ellie handed her rag off to another VAD and went immediately to Sister Lennox. She barely gave her a glance as she struggled with a man in extreme agitation. "Sing to him."

"What?"

"I've heard you before, singing to calm them. Please, sing to him."

Ellie looked at the soldier, arching violently off his cot as he gasped for air. A lullaby from her childhood came to mind, and she leaned close to his ear, singing and stroking his hand. He slowly stopped fighting and lay trembling, tears streaming from his eyes.

"Help me turn him," Sister Lennox said, and they positioned him with his head hanging over the side of his cot. Almost immediately, he coughed up great gobs of yellow gunk, which eased him. He lay back and immediately fell into an exhausted stupor.

"Thank you," Sister Lennox said, the strain evident in her face. Ellie nodded, and they fell into a tandem rhythm until, by the tireless efforts of the too small staff, all the men had been tended.

The nurses, orderlies, and VADs moved about, cleaning, feeding, and changing the dressings of hundreds of patients. Some of the more able-bodied wounded helped, God bless them, wiping down stretchers or spooning soup into the mouths of their weakened comrades. Ellie's last task before retiring, hopefully, was to restock the bandages on the ward carts. As she entered the dispensary, a nurse stood with head bowed, leaning on the shelving as if for support. The nurse's head shot up when she heard Ellie—it was Sister Lennox, who straightened and began tucking loose strands of her dark hair into her cap. Sister

Lennox's face was mottled and her large gray eyes shone with unshed tears. "Winthrop. You, ah, have completed your rounds, then?"

"Yes, Sister." Ellie was sorry to have barged in on her private moment, but concern loosened her tongue. "Are you all right?"

"Aye, of course." The strong, unflappable woman Ellie was used to had returned, but only for a moment. To her surprise, Sister Lennox's shoulders slumped, and with a deep sigh, she met Ellie's eyes. "I just...needed a minute. It's been a trying day."

The absurdity of the statement struck Ellie at the same moment as it seemed to strike Sister Lennox, and they laughed aloud. Every minute of every day was trying, but by God, Sister Lennox was smiling. They were both dirty, sore, and exhausted, but that smile lit Sister Lennox's face like a beacon in a storm. Ellie had always thought her beautiful, but standing there now, she was stunning.

After weeks of working side by side, they had developed into an efficient team, but Ellie barely knew her mentor. There was a chink in Sister Lennox's armor now, and Ellie threw caution to the wind.

"Sister Lennox, what is your given name?"

Her question was met by a look of surprise for a long moment, and then Sister Lennox answered quietly, "Johanna."

Perhaps it was Ellie's exhaustion that had her feeling cheeky. She stuck out her hand. "Pleasure to meet you, Johanna. I'm Eleanor, but you can call me Ellie."

Stifling a grin, Johanna clasped her hand. Her work-roughened skin was warm, her touch surprisingly gentle. "I'll do no such thing."

Ellie's heart dropped into her stomach and she pulled her hand away. *Bloody hell, I've overstepped my bounds.* She let out an audible groan of embarrassment.

"At least not while we're on duty."

Johanna winked, then stepped away and out of the room. Ellie stared after her, then shook her head with a smile. After all these weeks of insanity, she might have made the unlikeliest of friends. The thought somehow chased the day's troubles away.

❖

The next morning, Ellie received a parcel from England. Ignoring the cold, she stepped outside to open it in the fresh air. Inside was a tin of biscuits, a small pot of honey, a package of butterscotch candies, a pair of warm gloves, and a note from her father.

*My Dearest Ellie,*

*Your mother and I hope this arrives in time for Christmas. It's difficult to find much in the way of sundries these days, but we managed to gather one or two of your favorites. I'm sure you could use a touch of home, especially so near the holidays. We miss you and do hope you are taking good care of yourself. Write again to your mother—you know how she worries. Theo has not yet enlisted, but I don't know how much longer he'll wait. He has spoken of joining the medical corps instead of infantry to appease us. We shall see. Your mother will fill you in on all the gossip from home in her next letter. May God keep you safe, my dear.*

*With much love,*

*Papa*

Ellie opened the package of candies and popped one in her mouth, groaning at the rich, sweet flavor. Though the wonderful gifts had cheered her, this news of Theo was like a dark cloud obscuring the sun, and it saddened her no end. She knew full well that, if not a soldier, he could end up a stretcher bearer, fetching the wounded under fire in no-man's-land. The longer she was here, the more she felt that nothing would remain untouched by this war. Nothing would ever be the same. A group of mobile patients huddled nearby, smoking, their hospital blues like bright patches of cerulean sky amidst a dreary abundance of gray clouds. They laughed and chatted with their mates, desperate to regain their humanity, yet knowing as they healed that some would once again don khaki and face death. Ellie prayed that Theo would somehow stay safe.

She took the package to her sleeping quarters, then hurried back to the ward. The moments outside did little to rid her nostrils of the overpowering stench of a hospital at full capacity, nor her throat of its habitual soreness. She went about assisting with morning tea service for the men, dreaming of her own cup later with honey. A tap on her shoulder brought her face to face with Sister Lennox.

"You keep rubbing your throat," Sister Lennox said. "Try this." From her apron she pulled a small bottle and poured out two tablets, handing them to Ellie.

"What is it?"

"Formamint. It's for sore throat and helps a bit to mask the odors."

*Goodness, has she read my mind?* Ellie was quite surprised that Sister Lennox, with her immense workload, would notice something as inconsequential as her rubbing her throat. The little kindness warmed her.

"Thank you. You're very thoughtful," Ellie said, popping a tablet into her mouth. The taste of foul air immediately lessened.

"You're welcome, Miss Winthrop," Sister Lennox replied with a small smile, her gaze lingering on Ellie's face. After a moment, she blinked and stepped back. As Sister Lennox turned back to her work, Ellie remembered the treat she'd stashed in her apron pocket.

"Sister, wait. Let me return the favor." She pulled out a sweet and extended her hand in offering. Sister Lennox's eyes widened.

"Is that…?" She took the candy and placed it in her mouth, closing her eyes. "Oh, aye, butterscotch is my favorite. Thank you."

Ellie smiled at the blissful expression on Sister Lennox's face, feeling quite happy with herself that she'd thought to share. "It's my pleasure."

❖

There seemed no end to the wounded. No sooner did they empty a bed, than five more were ready to claim it. Johanna thought the volunteers were doing a splendid job, and most could change bed linens in a minute or two, thanks to Ellie, who had taken several of the VADs under her wing, teaching them to perform their duties in the most efficient way possible. She didn't know much about Ellie's background, but it was as if she was born to do this work. Even stodgy old Dr. Samuel had complimented her, and he criticized nearly everything.

Ellie. Johanna had taken to calling her that in her mind. It reminded her that they were women, not just workhorses in skirts. The name had a softness to it that calmed her, much like its owner. Johanna could tell she was high-born—most of the VADs were. She'd always thought such women were obnoxious and shallow, simpering and preening as they looked down their noses at people like her. Ellie had changed her assumptions, for she was smart, independent, strong, and kind. War had certainly reversed their roles, or at least brought them to common ground.

Johanna knew the others thought she was harsh and unfriendly—she wasn't an outgoing person by nature, and she was uncomfortable socializing with the nurses in their free moments. Yet she found herself, quite inappropriately, wanting to spend those moments with Ellie, who didn't seem to mind her unsociable ways one bit. It was a strange development, to be sure.

"Ambulances coming," an orderly yelled, startling her. She ran to help triage the wounded as they were unloaded, mentally inoculating herself to the gruesome task. The orderlies placed the stretcher cases on the ground in rows. Then they began the task of cutting away filthy, lice-ridden uniforms and washing the men before they could change their dressings or send them to the operating theater. Ellie appeared by her side, and they wordlessly bent to their work. Ellie had learned such a great deal and now anticipated what Johanna needed her to do. She was a balm for her nerves and a comfort to the men, and Johanna was grateful. She nodded to Ellie and was rewarded with a warm smile that somehow softened the jagged edges of their current reality. Taking a deep breath, she smiled back, feeling a bit more energized to handle the tasks at hand.

❖

It was one of those days, in between the frenzied rushes of wounded, when there was a lull and the staff had shorter shifts.

Ellie was off duty and restless—she'd already written to her parents, washed her clothes, and changed her bed sheets, and there was nothing left to do. Some of the girls passed the time with needlepoint and gossip, but that wasn't Ellie's style, and it was far too cold to walk about outside. After an early supper, she decided to head over to Ward A.

When she entered, she nodded to Sister Longley, who was just coming on duty. The clanging of metal bowls told her someone was working in the infirmary, but otherwise, the ward was calm and well-ordered. Since it was also warmer than her quarters, Ellie decided to stay for a bit. She checked on some of the more infirm patients who were awake, offering to write letters or read aloud, but none were interested. At the far end of the ward, four patients sat at a folding table, playing cards and trying to keep their competitive enthusiasm to a dull roar. Ellie smiled and headed their way.

"Good evening, gentlemen. Who's winning?"

"That would be me, miss," a young corporal answered. "These fine fellows here don't stand a chance."

"A bold declaration," Ellie said as the others grumbled. "What's the game?"

"Three-card brag," the corporal said, "for toothpicks." He indicated the sizable pile in front of him.

"Impressive. I was just thinking that I could use some more toothpicks—I'd be happy to take some off your hands, Corporal."

The other men hooted with laughter. "Deal her in, Johnny. Here, ma'am, you can have my chair," one said, and Ellie nodded with a smile.

"Thank you." Ellie sat down and listened politely as Johnny explained the rules, as if speaking to a child. "I think I understand now. Shall we begin?"

Johnny dealt a new hand with a cocky grin, but seven hands later, his grin was gone, as were half of his toothpicks. A small crowd of other patients had gathered and were cheering Ellie on as she put the young braggart Johnny in his place. She couldn't remember when she'd had such fun.

"Hallo, Sister," someone said, and Ellie looked up, expecting to see Sister Longley. Instead, she met the unreadable gaze of Sister Lennox.

"Miss Winthrop, what the devil are you doing?"

Ellie froze and a hush fell over the crowd of patients. Her mind scrambled for a reply. She was fairly certain she was allowed to play cards with the men. Still, she felt the blood rush to her face as she looked up at the imposing Sister Lennox.

One of the soldiers jumped to her defense. "Sister Sunshine was just having a bit of fun."

"Yes, I see that."

"I'm sorry, Sister," Ellie said. "I'm off duty, and…have I done something wrong?"

"Indeed you have. It seems you've taken advantage of this poor unsuspecting lad and swindled his toothpicks," she said with a wink.

Stunned, Ellie looked at Johnny, who was sitting back with his arms crossed, clearly feeling vindicated. She then looked back at Sister Lennox, whose eyes were twinkling with mischief. "My apologies," Ellie said, trying not to laugh.

"Perhaps you should give up your seat and let the corporal attempt to reclaim his honor."

"A fine idea, Sister Lennox," Ellie said, rising. "Thanks for the games, gentlemen." Leaving Johnny to his mates' ribbing, she and Sister Lennox donned their cloaks and stepped outside.

"You were drawing quite the crowd in there. Sister Longley didn't want to interrupt the fun, but the men need their rest," Sister Lennox said.

"Oh, I'm sorry," Ellie said, flushing hot at the gentle chastisement. "I didn't think."

"Quite all right." Sister Lennox cocked her head and gave Ellie a long look. "There certainly is more to you than meets the eye, Miss Winthrop. Good night."

She turned and walked away, leaving Ellie with the very same impression about the complex and unpredictable Johanna Lennox.

## CHAPTER SEVEN

It was Christmas morning, and they'd all just come from a lovely service, where all who were able sang hymns and prayed for peace. Last night Ellie had shared some of the biscuits and honey with her bunkmates—they'd moaned with every bite and yelled a cheery thank-you to her parents. Ellie wanted to share with Sister Lennox, but she'd been off on an errand for Matron since yesterday. She seemed rather melancholy of late—missing home at Christmastime, Ellie supposed.

It felt strange in the ward without Johanna Lennox. She was a presence, taller than the rest of the women and even some of the men. Ellie felt like there was order to their chaos when she was there, as if she, even more than Matron Campbell, was holding them all together. Quite odd, since many of the staff kept their distance from her. She'd heard them mutter, *She's so hard* or *That woman never smiles*. She didn't know why they judged Johanna so—this place made everyone ill-tempered at times. Ellie believed there was a story there, a different person underneath the harsh exterior. She was sure of it, because she'd witnessed the compassion in her eyes when tending the patients and because…she'd seen Johanna smile.

She preferred Johanna's company to that of most of the others she knew. Although many of the volunteers came from backgrounds similar to hers, she found she had little in common with them. Her bunkmates, Daisy, Mary, and Margaret, were all right, but Margaret mostly kept to herself, and the other two were a bit too gossipy and immature for her taste. Johanna was different than anyone she'd met before, more mature, more real. She wasn't pretentious, didn't put on airs or pretend to be someone she wasn't. Maybe it was Johanna's air of mystery that intrigued Ellie. She certainly admired her skills and expertise as a nurse, and her cool command was helpful in such a charged and stressful environment. At any rate, she saw something in Johanna that the others couldn't or didn't want to see.

❖

When Johanna got back to the hospital, it was quite late. She'd missed supper but just needed some hot tea to warm her. The night was windy and bitterly cold, and all she could think of was how the lads in the trenches could possibly survive it. She hurried to the kitchen, where the cooks kept hot water going all day and night. As she looked for a clean cup, the door banged open, startling her half to death. In came Ellie, carrying a basketful of hot water bottles to be filled. When she saw Johanna, a huge smile lit up her lovely face.

"You're back, thank goodness."

*Has Ellie missed me?* The thought made Johanna's insides flutter. "I'm sure you got along just fine without me."

"Only just," Ellie teased. "I have something I've wanted to give to you, a little Christmas gift, but I can't fetch it until these bottles are filled."

"Are you asking for my help?"

"I am if you want your present anytime soon." Ellie was still smiling, and her blue eyes twinkled. This friendly, lighthearted banter was just what Johanna needed.

She took a bottle and began filling it from the vat. "How was Christmas here?"

"Rather lovely, actually. Lots of singing and storytelling—even the German prisoners in Ward C joined in with their Christmas carols. One could almost forget for a moment that we're at war." Ellie's smile faltered. "God willing, we won't spend another Christmas like this one ever again."

"Aye, I sincerely hope not," Johanna said.

"What about you? Did you find a little Christmas cheer in your travels?"

"A bit. I went up to Number Fourteen at Wimereux to beg supplies. Their hospital is set up in a bonny seaside hotel, and the nurses decorated it with bits of red ribbon and pine boughs. It cheered the men a great deal."

"Did you sing with them?"

Johanna felt the familiar stab of pain in her chest. "I don't go in for much celebrating at Christmas."

"Oh no, why ever not?" When Johanna didn't answer, Ellie looked stricken. "I'm sorry, I've been far too bold with my questions."

Johanna had never shared her reason with anyone before—only her mother knew. But something in Ellie's eyes made her want to tell. "My brother Duncan was born on Christmas Day." She swallowed, blinking back tears. "He and my da ran a fishing trawler out of Leith. They were lost in an awful storm nigh on three years now."

Ellie somehow knew just what to do—she didn't fuss over Johanna or offer empty platitudes of sympathy. She simply laid a gentle hand on her arm and nodded. After a moment, Ellie said, "Your mother?"

"She's in Edinburgh now, a seamstress by trade. Last we spoke, she had joined a Red Cross working party, making bandages."

"Ah, vital work, that. Imagine trying to do our jobs without the help of those volunteers," Ellie said, patting Johanna's arm.

When Ellie removed her hand, Johanna felt the chill of its absence in a far deeper place than her skin. "Nae, I can't imagine," she said, but she wasn't thinking about her mother.

When they'd filled the water bottles, they left the mess tent together. Johanna was tired, but she wasn't quite ready to end her conversation with Ellie.

"I have to get these back to the ward," Ellie said, though she, too, seemed hesitant to part ways. "Your gift is in my hut. I can get it to you in the morning if you'd like to head off to bed. You must be exhausted."

"I'll walk with you. I should check in with Sister Claire now that I'm back." In truth, debriefing with Sister Claire could wait until morning, and sleep was beckoning, but for reasons she didn't have the energy to contemplate, she needed the kind, easy companionship Ellie provided.

They spent the necessary few minutes inside the ward, but as they headed out into the night, the headlamps of two motor ambulances pierced the darkness. Although they weren't on duty, they stood by as the orderlies unloaded the stretchers, in case they were needed. One of the drivers came around his vehicle and gasped.

"Ellie? Ellie Winthrop?"

Ellie squinted in the dim light, then her eyes opened wide in recognition. "Anna, is that you?"

"Yes! My God, it's good to see you." The driver strode forward and pulled Ellie into a bear hug. "I can't believe I've stumbled upon you—what great luck. How stupid we were, not planning how to keep in touch once we finished training."

"True, true. I've thought of you so often, and now here you are," Ellie replied, all smiles.

In the dark, Johanna had mistaken the figure for a man, with her cap and coat, but now she could see the long skirt of her ambulance driver's uniform. She watched as Ellie kissed the woman's cheek, then pulled her by the hand into the headlamps' glow. Johanna felt sick all of a sudden as she watched them hold hands and hug again, and she stepped back into the shadows, not wanting to witness the joyful reunion a moment longer. She hurried away to her quarters, upset and very confused.

❖

"Tell me how you've been getting on, Anna. Is your work terribly difficult?" Ellie asked, pulling Anna into the light.

"Well, I'd be lying if I said it wasn't, but we're so busy, I haven't the time to worry about it. I do find joy in helping, though, like I have a purpose. Do you know what I mean?"

"Yes, I know exactly what you mean. I feel as if I've changed so much—I'm not that naive girl who signed up for duty back in Lancashire, that's for certain," Ellie said.

Anna laughed. "Nor am I. Our mothers would faint from shock, seeing us now." She pulled Ellie into another hug. "I'm so glad you're well and safe. How is Theo? Has he joined up?"

Ellie shook her head. "Not yet, but it's only a matter of time, I'm afraid."

"I'll say a prayer for him, and now that I know where you are, I'll write. I so want to catch up, but I mustn't linger—there are always more wounded waiting to be picked up."

"Maybe you'll come back here again, then."

Anna shook her head. "Our unit is slated for transfer closer to Ypres. We'll have tea once we're home—that day will come soon, I hope."

Ellie nodded, tears in her eyes. "Go on, then, and be careful. I'll look forward to a good long chin-wag back in England."

"Until then, my friend," Anna said, climbing into the driver's seat of her ambulance. She waved and rumbled off into the night.

Ellie's chest hurt as both joy and sadness overwhelmed her. "Oh, Johanna, wasn't that something?" She turned back to the doorway, but Johanna was gone.

❖

"Good morning, Sister Lennox." Johanna turned as Ellie approached her, pushing the cart of dressings and bandages. Her lovely face was bright and cheerful, and Johanna felt drawn again, like a magnet to steel. She hadn't been able to get Ellie out of her mind last night as she'd tried to make sense of the unease she'd felt, seeing her with the ambulance driver.

"Good morning, Miss Winthrop," she said, nodding and turning back to her work.

Ellie came alongside her with the cart and began her preparations for this round of dressing changes. She was aware of Ellie's every move and couldn't help but steal glances now and then—at Ellie's smile, her incredible eyes, her hands as they gently assisted with the bandages and soothed the wounded men.

"Sister Lennox?"

Johanna jerked and felt her face heat as she realized she'd been caught staring at Ellie's hands. "Aye, uh, hand me those scissors."

Ellie complied and didn't say another word until they finished on that side of the ward, leaving Johanna to contemplate her own strange behavior. *What in the devil is the matter with me?*

After handing off the full bin of soiled bandages to one of the volunteers and replenishing the cart, Ellie rejoined her and broke the silence. "May I ask why you ran off last night? I had hoped to introduce you to my friend, but she couldn't stay."

"I was tired," Johanna said, her voice a bit too sharp. Cringing inwardly, she softened her tone. "That was your friend, then?"

"Yes, a family friend. Anna was betrothed to my cousin Charlie, and we joined up together after he was killed. She's living the dangerous life of an ambulance driver, so it was a blessing to see her safe and well. She's such a strong person— even two years ago, it would have been unheard of for a woman to drive an ambulance, never mind in a war zone."

Johanna nodded, feeling like a fool, unable for the life of her to understand why she'd reacted as she had. "I'm sorry about your cousin," she said.

"Thank you," Ellie said, then seemed to study Johanna intently, head cocked to the side. "Are you quite all right this morning? You seem...out of sorts."

Johanna's face heated once again, much to her annoyance. "Aye, I'm fine. We'd best finish up rounds before Dr. Samuel comes through."

"Yes, Sister." Ellie's hand on her sleeve stopped Johanna cold. "I just want you to know that I haven't forgotten our conversation from last night, or why the holidays are difficult for you. I'm happy to listen if you ever need to talk."

Johanna swallowed hard against the sudden lump in her throat and dared to meet Ellie's eyes. She saw genuine compassion in them, and when Ellie smiled, Johanna knew that despite her tendency to avoid personal connections, she very much wanted to accept the friendship being offered.

"That's very kind, Miss Winthrop. Thank you. Shall we carry on?"

Ellie removed her hand and nodded, her blue eyes sparkling as she smiled. "Of course."

❖

Alternating schedules meant Ellie used to have the hut mostly to herself on any given night, but now that had changed. Daisy and Mary moved to the day shift, so bedtime in the little hut was much too crowded when Ellie needed quiet time to decompress from the day's stress. Tonight the girls were giggly, as if they were at an adolescent sleepover, and Ellie was getting annoyed. She feigned sleep, not wanting to get pulled into their conversation.

"He told me about his home in Yorkshire," Mary was saying, "and he invited me to visit once we all get home. Do you think he really fancies me?"

"Yes, he certainly seems keen on winning your affections," Daisy replied.

"He asked me to meet him tomorrow night," Mary whispered. "He has to go back to his unit in two days and wants us to have some private time before he leaves. I think he wants to kiss me."

"That and more, I'm guessing. What will you do if he, you know…"

"He's going back to the war and could be dead in a week," Mary said, her voice quavering. "If he needs me to comfort him, I expect I will."

"Shh! Mary, you mustn't get caught. You'd be in big trouble, and so would he." There were muffled movements followed by several beats of silence, then more whispering.

"Do you think she's really asleep?"

"You'd better hope so. You know she's got Sister Lennox's ear. I bet she'd tell."

They settled down after that and eventually fell asleep. Ellie lay awake, thinking about Daisy's words. Daisy had her pegged all wrong—she wasn't a tattletale or a gossip. Mary's choices were her own, as were the consequences. But what did she mean about having Sister Lennox's ear? She tossed the question around in her mind for a while, but sleep claimed her before she could think of an answer.

*Her belly trembled with anticipation as she waited in the shadows of the orchard, the moonlight bathing the grounds in a bluish glow. This rendezvous was foolish and bold, but she didn't care. A symphony of night sounds surrounded her, and she closed her eyes, willing her heartbeat to calm.*

*"Ellie."*

*The voice of her dreams spoke quietly behind her, and gentle hands touched her shoulders. Though the air was cool, her body ignited at the first touch of lips on her neck. One arm came around her waist, pulling her close as the lips kissed and caressed her exposed skin, while the other hand slid down to cup her breast.*

*Ellie moaned and dropped her head back onto her lover's shoulder, reaching up to tangle her fingers in soft dark curls. "I need to kiss you," she said. Turning around, she traced her fingertips slowly along soft pale cheeks and full lips as she gazed into eyes the color of storm clouds. "Kiss me, Johanna."*

Ellie jerked awake, her body pulsing. She peered through the darkness, disoriented, for she could still smell the fragrance of her orchard at home, even as her eyes saw the walls of her hut in France. She felt as she had when she'd read Rose Talbot's book, but the throbbing down low was much stronger. Ellie pressed her hand between her legs and gasped as snippets of her dream floated across her consciousness, giving her glimpses of a beautiful, familiar face.

*Oh my God.*

The next day, Ellie felt as if every single person could read her thoughts, and she was deeply embarrassed. Her unease increased tenfold when Sister Lennox was around, which of course was often. She'd come to the conclusion that Daisy and Mary's conversation the night before, combined with her close working proximity to Sister Lennox and simple exhaustion, led her mind to concoct such a convoluted dream, because any other explanation was utter craziness…wasn't it? It didn't help matters that the almost-kiss of her dream stayed stubbornly in the forefront of her mind.

Ellie prided herself on her ability to handle difficult situations with relative aplomb, yet today, her nerves were getting the best of her. After she dropped the scissors for the third time during rounds, Sister Lennox sighed in exasperation.

"Miss Winthrop, you certainly have butterfingers today. What's got you so jittery?"

*You. My crazy, beautiful dream of you.* "I'm sorry, Sister. It's just…the cold. My fingers are stiff."

"Ah. Well, keep a hot water bottle handy and warm them whenever you get the chance. I need those hands of yours."

Ellie felt the blood rush to her cheeks. *Pull yourself together, for God's sake.* "Right, I'll do that. Thank you."

Johanna looked at her, eyebrow raised, for a few interminable seconds, then went back to her work.

Somewhere in the recesses of her exhausted mind, Johanna filed away some unnerving observations. Ellie Winthrop had been acting rather odd lately, as if she was nervous or embarrassed in Johanna's company. Over the past few months, Ellie had become a confident and efficient assistant on the ward and a leader among the other volunteers—in fact, Johanna relied on her a great deal. But in the last couple of days, the energy between them had shifted. She was acutely aware of Ellie when they were together, and even more so of her absence when they weren't. Was Ellie feeling the same?

One thing Johanna did know was that in this chaotic and emotionally painful existence, Ellie was a mainstay of calm compassion, a bright light in the dark. The steady stream of wounded men and their dire needs occupied most of Johanna's waking moments, leaving her little time or energy to contemplate her own jumbled feelings. All she knew for sure was that Ellie was a blessing.

## CHAPTER EIGHT

*Late March 1916*

They had made it through the worst of the winter, though not without cost. Many of the hospital staff suffered from chilblains on their feet, as it was impossible to truly get warm, and their hands were stiff and cracked. Still, they were far better off than the Tommies, who'd been losing parts to frostbite nearly as often as shrapnel these last weeks. As Ellie walked to the hospital from her quarters, she could almost imagine the warmth of spring in the air. Mack, one of the orderlies she worked with regularly, stopped her.

"Miss Winthrop, Matron Campbell has called a meeting," he said, "over there." Every available VAD and orderly stood along the outer wooden wall of Ward B, and she and Mack took their places among them.

"As you know," Matron began, "pneumonia and rheumatism have been on the rise. We're down four nurses, five orderlies, and eight volunteers to illness. I've asked for additional staff, but until then, we'll need to be working as efficiently as possible, round the clock. Beginning tomorrow, Sister Martin will be the daytime charge nurse for Surgical Wards A and B, and Sister Lennox will be in charge at night. They will be adjusting your shifts, and you will take any concerns immediately to them. I will oversee the facial and eye injury wards, and Sister Cameron has the infectious disease and gas wards. We are expecting an ambulance train tonight and must be sure all necessary items are readily at hand. That is all—you may return to your duties."

As Ellie turned to leave, Matron called, "Miss Winthrop, just a moment. You have a telegram."

She froze, staring at Matron Campbell as fear took hold. Telegrams were for bad news, weren't they? Oh God, was it her parents? Theo? She took the slip of paper from Matron's hand with a nod and slowly opened it, her fingers trembling.

*Hallo, Sis. Joined the RAMC just after Christmas. Heading to France next week with a field ambulance transport unit. Not cavalry, but still lots of horses. If near Boulogne, will send message. Be safe. Your Loving Brother, Lt. Theodore Winthrop*

Relief and worry warred in Ellie's head. Maybe he wouldn't be stuck in a trench, but he'd still be in danger. Nowhere here could be safe enough.

"Is everything all right, lass?"

Matron Campbell had stayed nearby and was looking at her with concern. Ellie was touched by her kindness. She smiled and shrugged, her eyes moist.

"I hope and pray that it will be, Matron. My little brother has joined the war."

❖

Ellie could feel Johanna's eyes on her as they changed the dressing on Private Smith's leg wound. She'd been picturing Theo in the face of every young soldier all morning, and it was playing on her emotional state.

"Something the matter?" Johanna murmured.

She glanced at Johanna and saw concern in her eyes. She wanted to confide in her—they'd spoken some about their families, and she'd told Johanna about Theo—but she felt guilty focusing on him when she was surrounded by so many other brothers, fathers, and sons.

She managed a small smile. "I'm fine." Johanna's expression told Ellie she wasn't convinced. Later that afternoon, Johanna pulled her aside in the dispensary.

"You've hardly been yourself all day. What is it? Can I help?"

Ellie threw up her hands and the words came tumbling out. "My brother joined up with the medical corps. He's probably on his way to a field ambulance unit somewhere. Clever devil found a way to incorporate his two great loves, horses and driving motor cars. But he's barely eighteen and a lieutenant— how in the world will he manage to lead men when he can't even remember to remove his muddy boots in the house?"

"Don't fash, Ellie. It will do you no good, nor him. It's a blessing that he's not a foot soldier."

By now Ellie was pacing. "But how can I not? Anything can happen in this godforsaken place." Her voice hitched, and Johanna put a hand on her shoulder to still her. She leaned into Johanna—they spent every day comforting their patients, but it had been a long time since she'd felt the soothing touch of another person. Johanna had softened considerably lately, at least toward her, and she was the only person Ellie wanted to be near when it all got to be too much. Just now, Johanna's kindness threatened to undo her, and she felt her eyes burn with tears. "I'm sorry. You're right, of course. Worrying changes nothing."

"No need for apologies. Pray for him, and send positive thoughts his way. That's all any of us can do." Johanna gave her shoulder a gentle squeeze and removed her hand. Ellie missed her touch immediately. "Let's finish up and get our supper. I begin on night shift tomorrow. Since you're the only one who tolerates my crusty Scottish charm, I've a mind to be selfish and schedule you with me."

Johanna's smile was teasing, but her eyes held a hint of something else. Hopefulness, perhaps?

"You are in charge, Sister Lennox," Ellie said, standing at attention and touching her fingers to her cap in a mock salute. "But if you're asking, I would be quite satisfied with the night shift."

Johanna's smile lit the room. "Good."

## CHAPTER NINE

*Two weeks later*

Johanna was damn near dead on her feet. It had been an extremely busy and difficult night, and she had just finished recounting events to Sister Martin when she was summoned to Matron's office. The door was ajar, so she knocked on the frame.

"Sister Lennox, please come in," Matron said.

"Good morning, Matron," Johanna said, stifling a yawn.

"Do sit down. I'm afraid I have some distressing news, lass."

Johanna felt an uncomfortable prickle at the back of her neck. "What is it?"

Matron took a deep breath and hesitated, and Johanna knew then that something terrible had happened. "A few days ago, German airships bombed Edinburgh and Leith, killing several citizens. The War Office sent this message to you."

Johanna couldn't move. After a moment, Matron said, "Shall I read it?" Johanna nodded, but she already knew.

*"We regret to inform you that on April 2nd, the evening of the German bombardment of Edinburgh, Mrs. Elizabeth Lennox*

*died due to heart failure, likely brought on by the shock of the event..."*

Matron's voice faded as a strange sort of buzzing sounded in Johanna's ears. She closed her eyes and tried to conjure the face she'd never see again. Mam was dead. Hands on her shoulders roused her, and she met the tear-filled eyes of Matron Campbell.

"Johanna, lass, I'm so very sorry. I've already arranged leave so we can get you home. Can you be ready in an hour?" Johanna nodded, but she was numb, too shocked even to cry. When she stood up, she felt off-kilter, as if she was on the deck of a boat in choppy seas. Matron took her arm to steady her, and they went together to Johanna's quarters.

"I've requested two weeks' leave, but if you need more time, please contact me," Matron said, as Johanna threw her few pieces of civilian clothing in her case. "I'm so terribly sorry, Johanna. Do take care."

"Thank you, Matron," she said, her own voice sounding distant and foreign.

She didn't really recall the drive to the station, nor much about her journey back to Scotland. She slept some, exhausted as she was, but her waking moments were filled with images of her mother, Da, and Duncan, too. Her entire family was gone. What was she to do now?

It was raining heavily when Ellie awoke, so she stayed in her quarters for a while, writing a letter to her parents. She'd been away from home less than six months, but it felt like an eternity. She indulged—or perhaps tortured—herself with images of her comfortable bed, her favorite chair in Papa's library, Cook's wonderful meals, even Mother's nagging that she hated so much. She could almost smell her mother's rose-scented perfume and the fragrant smoke from Papa's pipe. Her thoughts turned to Theo, riding Samson, his beloved chestnut stallion, or covered head to toe in mud from a rugby scrum with his mates, or his cheeky grin when he'd snatch the bacon off her breakfast plate. Now misty-eyed, she shook her head, put on her shoes and mackintosh, and headed to the hospital. Better to be useful than sit about wallowing in nostalgia.

She stopped in the mess tent to have a bite and looked around for Johanna. She wasn't there—hopefully she was still asleep, for last night had been dreadfully taxing. Ellie wasn't due to start her shift for a while yet, so she went into the ward to offer her letter-writing services to some of the more incapacitated men. Sean, a redheaded Irish boy, eagerly took her up on it, and she spent a good half-hour writing to his mum and fiancée. At the far end of the ward, she noticed Matron had come in and was speaking quietly to Sisters Martin and Cameron. She looked rather grim, and Ellie felt a shiver of unease crawl down her spine.

At the shift change, she went to the dispensary to gather the bandages they'd need to change the men's dressings. She so enjoyed assisting Johanna with this work—Johanna was an expert at dressing wounds and was always willing to teach little tidbits and tricks as they worked. When she returned to the ward, Sister Cameron was still there, but no Johanna.

"Ah, Winthrop, come on, then. We'll begin over here with this leg."

"Yes, Sister." Ellie brought over her bundle of supplies and gathered the soiled bandages as the nurse removed them. They tended to four patients before her curiosity got the best of her.

"Sister Cameron, forgive me, but where is Sister Lennox?"

She looked at Ellie sharply, as if she'd spoken out of turn. "Gone on leave, Matron said. Family emergency or some such. I'll be in charge now."

"Yes, Sister." They finished their rounds, but Ellie's stomach was knotted with worry. Johanna had only spoken of her mother back home—perhaps she had taken ill. Ellie went about her duties, but concern weighed heavily on her mind.

Private Williams, a cheerful and talkative chap, called her to him. In a loud whisper, he said, "What's got you so gloomy, Sister Sunshine?"

She shushed him and smiled, hoping Sister Cameron hadn't heard. She wasn't particularly tolerant of VADs in her ward and tended to treat them like servants. She would throw a bloody fit if she heard Ellie addressed by a title she had not earned.

"Stop calling me that, Private. You know I'm a volunteer." She pointed to her blue and white uniform. "See? No scarlet cape, no medal."

"I'll take you over her any day," he said, inclining his head toward Sister Cameron. "She's too much like my mum, and a crustier woman never lived."

Ellie shook a chastising finger at him but couldn't quite stifle a giggle. "Thanks for asking, but I'm fine." She straightened his blanket and moved on, resolving to put her concerns aside and be as upbeat as she could for the patients. She'd have time to worry about Johanna later.

She'd have many days, as it turned out. Ellie missed Johanna, and it wasn't just because she had to work with the pinch-faced taskmaster, Sister Cameron. It was really quite strange, surrounded as she was by dozens of people, but with Johanna gone, she felt alone. Maybe this place was beginning to drive her mad.

Ellie wanted so badly to know what had happened, but she felt it wasn't her place to ask Matron Campbell. She'd just have to wait until Johanna came back. Then the thought occurred to her—what if Johanna didn't come back? What if her family emergency kept her home for good? Such a distressing possibility made her stomach lurch.

A dozen new arrivals and rounds with Sister Cameron kept Ellie too busy to contemplate her feelings until later, when she lay in her bed, exhausted but too anxious to fall asleep. She thought of Johanna, of her beautiful face and the blue-gray eyes that telegraphed a vulnerability she tried so desperately to hide.

*It's perfectly understandable that I should want to support her, to care for her—is that not what friends do? Yes, of course it is. I did the same for Anna when she was in need.*

Lying there, she became aware that what her head was telling her and what her heart was feeling were two different things. She cared for Johanna, inexplicably, in a way she'd never cared for another. How could that be? Perhaps the intense bond she felt was due to this war, to the trauma of all they'd experienced together. This was a radically different reality to anything she'd known before, so it only made sense that her feelings would be different as well. As sleep finally claimed her, she convinced herself she'd found the answer, or at least one that made some sense.

## CHAPTER TEN

Five days. That's all it had taken for Johanna to pack away a life. It had been a shock to see the bomb-damaged building right next to her mother's home. The tenement on Marshall Street had seemed so very small when she went inside, the two rooms spare. Her mother's few possessions lay strewn about, some broken on the floor, and a layer of dust covered everything. Mam had sacrificed so much, had done everything she could to push Johanna on to a career, a better life.

"You'll not live in this place and work your fingers to the bone with nary to show for it," she'd said. "Your da and I, we're simple people—we chose to stick with what we knew. But you, my lovely, you are destined for greater things."

Johanna had been away for over two years, studying nursing and earning her living, but she never dreamed she'd miss the last years of her mother's life. How frightened Mam must have been, alone in the night when the bombs fell. Such thoughts had been Johanna's undoing these last days, but she could no longer wallow in her grief. This was not home with her family gone. She had nowhere else to go but back to France.

On the journey to Boulogne, a million thoughts and images crashed around in her head, but one kept coming to the forefront...

Ellie. She'd missed her, needed her calming presence more than once as she dealt with her mother's death alone. As much as she craved being near her, her head was telling her not to get close to another person, someone who would inevitably leave. All the loss she'd experienced, personally and professionally, felt like a millstone around her neck, weighing her down.

At the station, Johanna secured a ride on a motor ambulance bringing wounded to the hospital, and she asked a stretcher bearer for news.

"Men are still being injured or killed by the thousands, with no end in sight," he said, his voice resigned and bitter. "I've carried more men than lived in my entire village—it's madness."

Johanna patted his shoulder. "You're doing good work, Private. For all those men, I give you my thanks."

The young man nodded and looked away. Johanna's chest ached at the senseless brutality of it all, and she thought of the shell shock cases, men whose minds had shattered under the strain of fear. Maybe when it came down to it, death was a welcome escape. Such a thought was enticing in her present melancholy mood, but Johanna knew it wasn't the answer. Mam had always said that life was lived one step at a time, and no matter what came, one only had to worry about the next step forward. Johanna hoped that her memories, and her mother's words of wisdom, would sustain her.

It was midafternoon when Johanna sought out Matron Campbell. She'd come back sooner than expected, and Matron was surprised to see her.

"Sister Lennox, my goodness, why back so soon? I can't say I'm sorry to see you—you've been sorely missed. How are you managing?"

"Nothing left to be done but my duty, Matron," Johanna said, avoiding her sympathetic gaze. She had carefully patched herself back together and would not fall prey to talk of feelings. "I will be ready to resume work at the shift change."

"Well, all right then, if you're sure. You are most certainly needed. I'll have Sister Cameron debrief you shortly. Is there anything you need, Johanna?"

"Nae, and thank you, Matron." She couldn't trust her voice to say more than that, and she quickly took her leave. In her quarters, a quick change of clothes had her ready to put the last week behind her. *One step at a time, Mam...I'll do my best.*

When Ellie saw the tall, slim figure in the center of the ward, her heart skipped a beat. She had her back to her, talking to a rather put out looking Sister Cameron, who, moments later, walked out the door. Johanna slowly turned, and when their eyes met, Johanna's raw, pained expression hit Ellie like a blow. She had the insane desire to run and gather Johanna in her arms, to soothe away the pain that marred her lovely face. She watched as Johanna took a deep breath, straightened her shoulders, and nodded.

"Miss Winthrop, would you fetch the bandages, please?"

Ellie felt as if she'd been slapped. She was sure she'd seen her own feelings mirrored in Johanna's eyes until that mask of indifference slammed into place. Awareness of the patients and staff all around brought Ellie to her senses. She had a job to do.

Silence reigned as they fell into their usual rhythm. Ellie reveled in Johanna's presence, so happy to have her back, but the space between them was tainted with awkwardness and uncertainty. *Why is she so distant? What happened in Scotland to change her so?* She would have to wait for answers—the war had come knocking once again.

Orderlies and stretcher bearers burst through the door with the first of a massive batch of wounded. Sister Lennox sprang into action, triaging and delegating, and hours passed before Ellie could catch her breath. Most of the men had shrapnel wounds or trench foot, and they raced against sepsis, washing away blood and grime as soon as the nurses had cut away the soiled, foul-smelling uniforms and bloody field dressings. The bits of cloth, dirt, stone, and metal embedded in the flesh were the enemy. Wounds were washed with carbolic lotion while doctors in the operating theater debrided and repaired the torn bodies as best they could, finishing the hasty work done in the field ambulances and amputating what they couldn't save. Body after body passed through the surgery, the five operating tables in constant use until the doctors nearly collapsed from exhaustion.

Ellie's feet and back were on fire, her hands so stiff she could barely grasp a bandage, yet all one could do was keep on. She thought she'd been sufficiently inured to this work, but the heartache for these boys whose lives had been tragically, irreparably altered threatened to consume her, and there were sights her eyes could never unsee. Yet there was nothing to be done for it, so they all just continued, minute by minute, to meet the next greatest need. When things slowed enough for their relief to take over, the staff stumbled off for whatever rest or sustenance they could find.

Ellie walked out into the fine spring morning and stood for a moment, relishing the warmth of the sun on her face. She was physically exhausted but too mentally worked up to sleep just yet. The sea called to her, and she answered. As soon as she reached the beach, she removed her shoes and stockings and gathered up her skirt, then walked gingerly to the water's edge. As the seawater washed over her burning feet, she groaned aloud. She stood in the numbing cold until the throbbing pain subsided. Some minutes later, Ellie turned to find she wasn't alone.

❖

Ellie stood in the surf, head and feet bare, the sun catching the reds and golds in her hair. Johanna wanted to go to her, to apologize for being a horse's arse earlier, before the wards had been overrun with wounded. But then what? The push and pull of her was driving Johanna crazy. How could she want to be close to this woman when she was so afraid? As her thoughts battled in her head, Ellie turned and saw her, stood for a long moment, then raised a tentative hand in greeting. Johanna couldn't leave now.

Ellie beckoned and began to walk away from the main path that led back to the hospital. Johanna followed her as she headed toward the cliff side, to a natural alcove of rock tucked in amidst the beach grasses. No one else was in sight.

"I found this little hideaway last week," Ellie said. "Sitting here watching the sea, I can pretend we're not at war, at least for a moment or two."

"Ellie, I'm sorry," Johanna said. Ellie stepped close and put a finger to her lips, shushing her.

"The water must have called you, as it did me. Just listen to the waves."

As Johanna stood there, eyes closed, profound exhaustion overcame her, and she swayed on her feet. She felt a hand on her arm, steadying, calming. She opened her eyes and gazed into brilliant blue depths that she fancied could see into her soul, which both frightened and exhilarated her.

"Are you all right?" Ellie asked.

"Aye, I think so. Last night was rough. A week away made me soft, I reckon."

"Were you able to sort out your family emergency?"

The question pierced Johanna's heart. "Family emergency?"

"Yes," Ellie replied. "Sister Cameron said that's why you were granted leave."

*My God, no one knows.* Johanna shook her head. "Edinburgh was bombed by German zeppelins nearly a fortnight ago," she whispered. "My mother..."

Ellie's hand flew to her mouth. "Oh, Johanna. Was she...?"

Johanna nodded. "She must have been so bloody scared— her heart just gave out." Her face grew hot as all the tears she'd been holding back demanded release. She turned away, fighting for control, her eyes squeezed shut. She couldn't look at Ellie, her beautiful face so full of compassion. She couldn't bear it if...

And then she was in Ellie's arms. Ellie held her close and the dam burst. She cried and cried, for Mam and Da and Duncan, for the dead soldiers and devastated survivors, purging years of grief and pain. She buried her face in Ellie's neck, in her soft, soft hair, and let it all go. Ellie rubbed her back and smoothed her hair, murmuring words of comfort. When Johanna could breathe, her fear found its voice.

"I have no one left now. I'm all alone."

Ellie pulled back and took her face in her hands, her thumbs gently smoothing the tears away. "You have me, Johanna."

Johanna saw then that Ellie was crying, too, and her heart clenched painfully in her chest. "Nae, lass, I didn't mean to distress you." Ellie's tears nearly shattered her.

"Shh, shh." Ellie leaned close and kissed Johanna's cheek, then the other, their tears mingling.

"Ellie." Ellie's eyes were full of compassion, but Johanna saw something else that drew her in. Unable to stop herself, she slid her hand through Ellie's hair, cupping the back of her head. Ellie's arms tightened around her, and Johanna kissed her.

The rest of the world fell away as Johanna basked in the wonder of soft lips caressing hers, igniting a passion she'd never felt before. Need bloomed in her depths and she deepened the kiss, tracing Ellie's bottom lip with her tongue, then plunging into her sweet mouth. Ellie welcomed her, meeting her tongue with thrusts of her own. Ellie's hands slipped into her hair and held her there, until Johanna could scarcely breathe. When she pulled her mouth away, Ellie whimpered, and Johanna's eyes flew open. Suddenly aware of their surroundings, she hastily scanned the beach. Had anyone seen them?

"Oh my God," Ellie breathed, staring at Johanna in shock, her fingers touching her swollen lips.

*What the bloody hell was I thinking?* Johanna's pulse thudded as the implications raced through her brain. She had kissed a woman, which in itself was enough for dismissal, or worse. She'd also crossed the line professionally, taking advantage of a subordinate, and putting her in jeopardy as well. *Damned fool—I was so wrong to let myself need her.*

"I'm so sorry," Johanna whispered, backing away. Ellie's face was flushed, her eyes wide, and Johanna just couldn't stand it.

"Johanna," Ellie said, reaching out, "I—"

"Stop," Johanna said, more forcefully than she intended. Swallowing, she tried again. "Nae, Ellie, I should not have let this happen. I'm a fool, and I'm so, so sorry." Ignoring Ellie as she called her name, she ran back to the hospital as fast as her tortured feet would carry her.

## CHAPTER ELEVEN

B andage-rolling duty was exactly what Ellie needed—
mindless work that left her free to think. Not that
thinking was getting her anywhere. How could the single most
incredible moment of her life cause such turmoil? *That kiss, my
God*...It was on her mind constantly, and she'd tried desperately
to sort out her feelings. Unfortunately, the one person she needed
to talk to was avoiding her like the plague.

*She's pawned me off on the other nurses, and if we must
be near one another, she can't look me in the eye. I know she's
tormenting herself about what we did, but was it truly a mistake?*

Back at home, several young men had tried to catch Ellie's
eye, either of their own accord or because of her mother's
incessant attempts to marry her off. A few were bold enough to
kiss her cheek and try for more, but the most she'd ever felt was
flattered. More often than not, their attempts were annoying or
downright offensive. Why, then, did kissing this woman leave
her wanting so desperately?

Ellie wasn't naive—it was no secret that there were women
who had relationships with other women. There was talk about
the suffragists and feminists, she knew, rumors that some of
the women were *that way*. She thought about her long-ago

conversation with Rose Talbot, who had told her about the writings of women like Gertrude Stein and Sappho. Ellie had only had the chance to read a few pages of the book she had borrowed, but she remembered the author had written about the kinds of feelings she was now experiencing. And then there'd been that dream months back, when she'd awakened with her body aroused and wanting. Had she felt a subconscious desire even then to kiss Johanna?

She wondered now why Rose had spoken to her of such things. It had certainly been risky—Rose couldn't have predicted how Ellie would respond. Did Rose sense something in Ellie that she herself hadn't realized? She thought she'd understood and accepted such relationships on an intellectual level, but never had she felt the emotional or physical pull of a woman, until now. What did it all mean?

The moments on the beach with Johanna came on the heels of a frightfully difficult night. They'd both been pushed to their physical and emotional limits in the hospital, and Johanna was overcome with grief, besides. Perhaps they were just in need of comfort. And yet, that comforting embrace led to kissing, and… Ah, Ellie's head was dizzy with uncertainty.

The door banged open and she jumped, nearly dropping the bandage she'd been rolling. Her face instantly heated at the sight of Johanna standing in the doorway, as if she had been pulled in by Ellie's swirling thoughts. Her heart leapt but just as quickly sank at the look on Johanna's face.

❖

*For the love of Christ…must she be everywhere?* Johanna's heart thudded as she looked at Ellie, her lovely face anxious and sad. She hated that she was the cause of Ellie's pain, but she had to be strong.

"I, uh, just needed some lotion," she said, then looked away, irritated at herself. She would not have explained her presence to anyone else, but this woman had her dangerously off-kilter. It was maddening. She walked quickly to the shelves and grabbed a crock of carbolic, then spun around to leave.

"Wait."

The plaintive tone of Ellie's voice stopped her cold, but she couldn't bring herself to look at her.

"Johanna, please, can we talk?"

Johanna took a deep breath to steel herself, then turned to face the woman who had upended her world. Ellie had abandoned her task and come closer, her eyes shimmering with unshed tears.

"Why are you avoiding me? It's so much harder to get through the day when you won't speak to me. I thought we were friends," Ellie said, tears spilling.

It took everything Johanna had to harden her heart. "We cannot be friends, Miss Winthrop. I was wrong to think otherwise."

"But why?"

Her chest tightened. "I think you know."

Ellie threw her hands in the air. "For God's sake, why can't you just forget the beach and go back to the way things were?"

"Can you forget?" The parade of emotions that crossed Ellie's face told Johanna the answer. "This is best for both of us."

Ellie's cheeks flushed as her temper flared. "Now you claim to know what's best for me?"

"Aye, Miss Winthrop, I do." Johanna walked out of the dispensary, closed the door behind her, and somehow went on about her work. She knew she was right to distance herself from Ellie, but her leaden heart would need some convincing.

An hour later, Johanna received a summons to Matron Campbell's office. Anxiety prickled along her spine as she remembered the last time she'd been called there, but she didn't have to worry about bad news any longer—she had no one left to lose. She stepped inside, looking curiously at the others gathered in the room.

"Sisters," Matron Campbell said to the six nurses standing before her, "Dr. Albert sent word that more nurses are needed at Hazebrouck, and they're reassigning staff from the base hospitals. The wounded are coming in faster than the casualty clearing stations can handle, and they've asked for two of my most experienced nurses. It will be a temporary assignment, two to three months, and much closer to the front. Therefore, I'll ask for volunteers."

Matron stood silently as they looked at each other. Johanna thought about what a CCS would be like and wondered briefly if she had the nerve to handle such a place, but then her mind jumped to Ellie. Being around each other had been tense and difficult—this would be her chance to put some physical distance between them, for both their sakes. Her mind made up, Johanna took a deep breath, looked at Matron Campbell, and raised her hand.

❖

Johanna had entered a whole new level of hell. She thought she'd seen the worst of what this war would bring, but her experiences had barely scratched the surface. From dusk to dawn, the field ambulances brought a constant stream of wounded men, many of whom looked barely human. Her senses were battered by noises and smells and horrific sights, and the urge to flee was strong, but it was their eyes that held her fast. These husbands and brothers and sons, at least those that still could see, looked at her with such trust, patiently waiting for relief from their torment. She could not let them down.

The CCS consisted of several large white canvas tents, each with its own purpose. Abdominal cases, amputees, head cases, infectious diseases, the gassed ones—they all had their place. Stretchers lined the ground outside, so close together that one could barely step between them. Their occupants waited to be triaged and treated, while walking wounded sat nearby. The critical cases, many of whom had lain for hours on the battlefield before they were found, were so numerous that many died before the medical staff could get to them.

In the near distance Johanna could hear the guns, and every inch of her ached from the toil and tension. She and Sister Claire were on triage, sorting the men by their wounds, while others removed filthy, lice-infested uniforms and washed the men up for the surgeons. Too often, she called the poor overwhelmed chaplain for those whose lives were quickly ebbing away. The stretcher bearers and orderlies worked until they could barely stand, but their much-needed rest rarely came. Johanna's world became a blur of mud and blood, the stench of long-unwashed bodies and decaying flesh matched only by the miasma of pain and despair that hung over the place.

For nearly three straight days, thirty doctors, nurses, and orderlies dealt with over a thousand wounded, doing everything humanly possible to spare as many lives as they could. Despite their best efforts, the small wooden crosses in the station's graveyard multiplied by the hour. Finally, a lull in the fighting gave them a chance to catch their breath.

Johanna stumbled to the nurses' hut, absently noting that Claire was already there, fast asleep. She was barely able to remove her soiled uniform before collapsing on her own narrow cot. Amazingly, sleep didn't come right away. As she tried to calm her mind, an image came to her of a lovely woman with strawberry-blond hair and eyes as blue as a summer sky. Focusing on Ellie's smile, she drifted into a blessed, dreamless sleep.

It was as if a wee invisible Ellie had stowed away in Johanna's pocket to be with her at Hazebrouck. Johanna's mind and soul were bombarded daily with desperation and pain, but in her most difficult moments, memories came to sustain her— Ellie's smile that lit up her face like sunshine, her sweet clear voice that calmed and comforted, her gentle touch. She thought about how the men perked up when she came around to care for them, and her unfettered delight in the simple things, like butterscotch sweets or winning a game of cards. But it was the things she'd resolved to put behind her—Ellie's warm embrace and the sweet taste of her lips—that now tethered her to sanity.

# CHAPTER TWELVE

*Ten weeks later*

Sister Claire was dead. They'd traveled together to that godforsaken clearing station, worked night and day until they could barely move, and somehow managed to get through it. She'd told Johanna about her home, her family, the young man she hoped to marry one day. She was a kind and lovely soul.

Their return to No. 7 and the end of their nightmare in Hazebrouck was so close, but life was cruel. Two days before they were to transfer back to Boulogne, an artillery barrage hit one of the surgical tents, killing a doctor, two nurses, and twenty-seven wounded soldiers. Sister Claire was dead, and Johanna felt broken beyond repair.

As the train crawled the forty miles to Boulogne, she thought about her life before France. Decades ago, it seemed, when she was blissfully unaware of what was to come. Her exhausted brain was bombarded with memories—Da, his feet propped up by the fire, drinking a dram or three of whiskey after a long day on the boat; Mam repairing a rich woman's torn gown, her rough fingers reddened from a thousand needle sticks; Duncan begging to skip school so he could go fishing. The scenes were so vivid, she could almost reach out and touch them—those dear ones, the center of her life, were gone. Johanna could barely remember who she'd been then, before a heartless sea took her father and brother, and before her heartbroken mother had unselfishly begged her to seek a better life.

Johanna had made her choice, and it had brought her here, a witness to the barbaric destruction of war. Sleep was fractured now, her mind unable to rest because of all her eyes had seen and hands had touched. It had become harder to conjure the memories that sustained her—the comforting arms that had pulled her close, kiss-swollen lips and eyes alight with wonder. Johanna could no longer deny her feelings. She needed Ellie as one needed air, but the unknown tortured her. Was Ellie still there? Would she forgive Johanna for pushing her away, for leaving?

Ellie was walking to the mess tent when the supply truck lumbered through the far gate. She stopped to watch the orderlies unload it, hoping their emergency requisitions had arrived. Her heart skipped a beat when a familiar figure in a nurse's uniform stepped out of the vehicle. *Oh my God...Johanna?* Ellie started to run to her, to see for herself that she was all right, before her brain kicked in and stopped her in her tracks. *Will she even want to see me?* She'd left weeks ago, volunteered, the others said, to be closer to the front. Ellie knew Johanna's character—she was an excellent nurse and would never hesitate to help where she was needed, but part of her was convinced that Johanna left to get away from whatever had happened between them.

As Johanna grabbed her bag and walked toward Matron's office, Ellie felt weak with relief. She'd prayed and prayed for Johanna's safe return, knowing now the depth of her feelings. She'd convinced herself that she could handle the loss of their friendship as long as she knew Johanna was safe. Now, she wasn't so sure. Still, Ellie would leave it up to her. She turned, and though the effort felt like pushing against a raging current, she walked the other way.

Later, as Ellie began her shift, Mack came up to her. He was her favorite orderly and a bit of a gossip.

"Sister Lennox is back, you know," he said. "Heard she's having a rough time of it, what with Sister Claire getting killed."

Ellie's blood ran cold. "What?"

"Yeah, those bloody Germans shelled the place. Thought you knew. Imagine, those poor blokes getting hit in the trenches and living long enough to get blown to bits in a hospital tent. Can't make no sense of this goddamn war, and you'll pardon my language, miss."

Mack droned on about this and that, but Ellie barely heard him. Sister Claire was dead, the poor soul. Had Johanna been near the attack? She had to be distraught. Ellie went about her tasks, trying to focus on the patients, but the need to check on Johanna was overwhelming. Ellie was due to go on leave in two days—she had to figure out a way to speak to her before then.

❖

The summer sun was blazing by the time Ellie finished up her shift and stepped outside. She could almost forget the long winter months when she thought she'd never be warm again. She needed to rest but knew the atmosphere in her hut would be oppressive. Grabbing a spare blanket, she headed down to her little cubbyhole by the sea.

The breeze off the water soothed Ellie instantly, and she breathed deeply, taking the fresh air into her lungs. She thanked God for the hundredth time that she'd been sent to a hospital on the coast, for the ocean did more to restore her than anything else. A handful of soon-to-be-discharged convalescents splashed in the waves, laughing and enjoying themselves before being shipped off again to God knew where. Ellie turned away from them and headed back toward the cliff. As she neared her spot, she heard a keening sound, high-pitched and eerie. Her heart hammered in her chest as she stepped slowly around the curve in the rock face.

Johanna was sitting on the sand in civilian clothes, her arms hugging her bent knees. Eyes closed, her tearstained face was raised to the sky as she rocked back and forth, sobbing. Ellie's head told her to leave, to give her the privacy she'd clearly sought, but her heart broke in the face of such pain. Risking her displeasure, Ellie walked slowly to Johanna, knelt at her back, and gently embraced her. Johanna's breath caught, but she said nothing.

"I'm here," Ellie whispered. "I know your pain is deep, but you don't have to bear it alone. Please don't push me away."

Johanna, as if she had no fight left, laid her head back on Ellie's breast, letting herself be held as she cried. After a while, Ellie eased down to sit beside her, rubbing Johanna's back as she regained her composure.

"I'm so sorry about Sister Claire," Ellie said, even while knowing her simple words would never be enough.

Johanna took a deep shuddering breath and picked up a handful of sand, letting it slowly sift through her fingers. "She did so much good. She wasn't even assigned to that tent, but another nurse had taken ill." Ellie jumped when Johanna pounded both fists into the sand. "Doesn't it seem as if the Fates are just playing with us, taking this one and sparing another? Sister Claire didn't deserve that. It should have been me."

Ellie was alarmed at the vehemence of Johanna's words, but she didn't contradict them. She understood Johanna's anger and despair, and somehow she knew that Johanna had to move through this pain if she was ever to heal.

"I've given up on trying to make sense of this war," she said after a moment. "But if it's fate that determines our destiny, I can only believe that you were spared for a reason. I, for one, am beyond grateful."

Johanna turned to look at Ellie then, doubt clouding her eyes. "I know I hurt you, and yet here you are. Why?"

"That's a conversation for another time," Ellie replied, reaching over to tuck a wayward strand of hair behind Johanna's ear. "For now, I just need to know that you're all right."

Johanna nodded, capturing Ellie's hand in hers. Ellie entwined their fingers, feeling weak with relief. "I'm going on leave tomorrow, to Paris," she said, "but I don't want to walk away from you now."

Johanna searched Ellie's face, and Ellie prayed she could see her truth in her eyes. "You won't have to," Johanna said. "I'm not expected back on duty for three days."

Ellie's heart soared in disbelief. "Truly? Why, then you could…"

"Aye. Let's go to Paris."

## CHAPTER THIRTEEN

Serendipity…was that the word? Johanna wondered. Whatever it was, she and Ellie had been granted three days' leave at the same time. Two other VADs from their hospital were on the train with them, and they kept up appearances, sitting across from each other and engaging in mundane chatter. Johanna knew, though, when Ellie caught her eye, that Ellie wanted them to be alone as much as she did.

When they reached Paris, the others went on their way, and Ellie and Johanna caught a streetcar to their destination.

"Look," Ellie said, jerking her chin toward the front of the car. "The driver is a woman."

Her excitement was infectious, and Johanna couldn't help smiling. They got off the streetcar at the appointed stop and walked a block to a small hotel. There was a café on the ground floor, the rooms on the three floors above.

"Would you like to get a coffee?" Johanna asked, suddenly nervous. The idea of being truly alone with Ellie had her stomach in knots.

"That would be lovely," Ellie said, her face lighting up. "It's bound to be better than what we get in the mess."

They sat at a small ornate iron table, their bags at their feet. Johanna ordered two coffees, lightened with milk the way the

French liked it. They sipped the beverages and looked around at their little corner of Paris. Ellie exclaimed with delight over the little things—a planter of colorful pansies by the café door, an old man whistling as he rode by on his bicycle, the bold pigeon that hopped over and pecked her shoe. Johanna was charmed by Ellie's youthful enthusiasm, and she couldn't take her eyes off her.

Ellie looked more at ease without her uniform on, as if civilian clothes removed a weight from her shoulders. Her dress was a lovely peach color that complemented the subtle shades of her hair and the cream of her complexion. She'd put on some lipstick, the lively color drawing Johanna's eyes to her mouth. She'd never looked at a woman, noticing all the finer details, as she did now with Ellie. She was so very beautiful.

"What?" Ellie said, one eyebrow quirking up.

"Just appreciating the view," Johanna said, watching Ellie's cheeks flush in response to her boldness.

"You flatter me. You're looking quite lovely yourself."

Johanna looked down at her sage-green dress. Her mother had made it as a going-away gift before she left for training in London. Johanna had scolded her for spending too much on the fabric, and the memory pained her now.

"Johanna? What is it?"

"This dress was the last thing my mother gave me," she said, avoiding Ellie's eyes. She drained the rest of her coffee and stood, nearly knocking over the table. She would not cry in public. "I'll go check us in."

She felt Ellie behind her as she stood at the hotel desk. The concierge looked them over, then handed Johanna the room key. "Merci," she said. Glancing at Ellie, she headed for the lift that would take them to their third floor room.

They didn't speak a word until they'd entered the room. Ellie put her bag at the foot of the closest twin bed and turned to her.

"Are you all right, Johanna?"

The gentle way Ellie said her name nearly started her crying. She nodded, not trusting her voice.

Ellie looked at her for a long moment, then sat on the edge of the bed, smoothing her hands over the chenille bedspread. "This will feel like heaven tonight, but I've got to have a proper bath first."

"What about dinner?" Johanna said, regaining her voice.

"I'm perfectly happy with room service, if you are."

Johanna nodded, relieved. She didn't want to be around other people tonight. "Go ahead with your bath. I'll find the menu and order us something."

Ellie smiled as she rummaged around in her bag. She pulled out a nightgown and disappeared behind the heavy curtain that separated the bedroom and bathroom. Johanna hunted around for a menu and, finding none, rang the concierge. He gave the meal choices, apologizing profusely for the limited fare that strict rationing had forced. Twenty minutes later, the food arrived. Ellie had still not emerged from the bath.

"Ellie, our dinner is here." When she didn't respond, Johanna called out again, then eased the curtain aside. Ellie was reclining in the claw-foot tub, head resting on the edge, sound asleep. A mixture of tenderness and desire washed over Johanna, leaving her breathless. The water came to just above Ellie's waist, leaving her pale breasts exposed. Johanna looked away, face hot, and grabbed a towel.

"Ellie, wake up, lass," she said, holding up the towel as a barrier. She heard a gasp and the splash of water.

"Oh my goodness, I fell asleep. I'm sorry, Johanna. The water was so warm, and I—"

"Don't fash, Ellie. Come now...our food is getting cold." More splashing, then Ellie took the towel and wrapped it around her body. She looked at Johanna, face flushed, tendrils of wet hair a darker red against her porcelain skin.

"Thank you," she said, glancing away. Johanna stepped back, fighting the urge to pull Ellie's clean, warm, lavender-scented body into her arms.

"I'll, uh, leave you to dress, then." Johanna quickly stepped around the curtain, her body buzzing like a live wire. She'd always viewed a nude body in a clinical, detached sort of way, but the sight of Ellie's loveliness stirred up feelings she'd never experienced before.

Ellie emerged wearing a white bathrobe, a small luxury the hotel had provided. They dined on a savory fish and vegetable stew with thick slices of brown bread. "Mmm," Ellie said, moaning between mouthfuls. "This is perhaps the best meal I've ever eaten."

"Somehow I doubt that," Johanna replied, smirking. "Not everyone has their own personal chef."

"Nor do I," Ellie said, lifting her chin in defiance. "Cook has been with our family since my father was a boy, but she isn't a trained chef."

"And does this cook have a name?"

"That is her name," Ellie said, trying to keep a straight face.

"Mrs. Cook the cook?"

"Exactly."

Johanna laughed, and Ellie joined in, their fit of giggles relieving some of their tension.

After supper, Johanna took her own bath. The lavender soap was a luxury she'd never had, and she inhaled deeply, the fragrance delightful. Once the water began to cool, she got out and dressed in a simple cotton shift. When she re-entered the bedroom, her pulse quickened. Ellie had removed her robe and now sat on the bed in a pale pink embroidered nightie. The silky fabric clung to her body, and she'd never looked more lovely. Johanna glanced down for a moment at her own garment, feeling like a peasant wearing a potato sack. Ellie didn't seem to mind—she bit her lip, her gaze traveling quickly over Johanna's body before meeting her eyes. Dismissing her sudden urge to kiss Ellie as too bold, Johanna sat on the other bed. Her hands clenched the coverlet as she studied the floor.

"Ellie, I know we have much to talk about, but I've no bloody notion where to begin."

"Well, we could start simply and discuss the weather," Ellie said with a smile.

"That's easy. It's hot," Johanna replied.

"And are you satisfied with our accommodations this evening?"

Johanna laughed. "Compared to what I've slept in lately, this is the Ritz."

"Hmm, all right then, I think I must move to more serious topics," Ellie mused, tapping her chin with a finger. Her smile faded as she regarded Johanna intently. "Why did you volunteer for the CCS?"

Johanna had known this was coming, but she worried that if she told the truth, there'd be no going back. "I needed to get away, to clear my head." She felt the weight of Ellie's gaze, but she couldn't look at her.

"Away from me?"

"Och, I don't know." Johanna stood and went to the window, willing herself to calm down as she watched the people below, bustling around before the coming darkness forced them inside.

"Johanna," Ellie said, coming behind her and laying a hand on her shoulder. Johanna trembled at her touch and knew she could no longer hide her feelings.

"It's wrong of me to want you," Johanna said, her voice low. She placed her palms on the windowsill, for if she turned around, there would be no more talking. "Fraternization aside, what good could come from us being together? I'm not from your world. Your family—"

Ellie tightened her grip on Johanna's shoulder and spun her around, silencing her protests.

"I don't give a damn what anyone thinks, Johanna," she said, eyes flashing. "I know what I'm about, and I know my feelings for you are too wonderful to be wrong. Tell me you didn't miss me while you were gone. Tell me I didn't cross your mind."

Those words took away the last bit of Johanna's strength, and she touched her forehead to Ellie's. "My God, Ellie, you have no idea. When I was out there, it was so horrible." Her voice broke as she shuddered. "Thinking of you was the only thing that kept me sane."

Ellie brought a hand up to cup Johanna's cheek as tears streamed down hers. "I prayed and prayed that you would be safe, that I would see you again," she whispered. "Now you're here, and I don't ever want to let you go."

Johanna pressed her lips to Ellie's forehead. "Don't cry, dearest. I can't bear to see you cry." She smoothed Ellie's hair with a gentle hand, then tipped up her chin to gaze into her eyes. "I feel so much with you. It's as if you soften everything in me that the war has hardened. I can't explain how or why—I just know that you fill up a place I thought could never be filled." She stroked her thumbs softly across Ellie's tearstained cheeks. "This need I have for you, it frightens me. Are you frightened, too?"

Ellie shook her head. "The only thing that frightens me is the thought of losing you. Fate, I think, has brought us together for a reason, my darling. And," she said, taking a half step closer, "if you don't kiss me, I may die from the wanting."

Johanna gathered Ellie into her arms and claimed her mouth with a groan. Ellie matched her intensity, caressing and tasting, and then opened for her, their tongues colliding in a feverish dance of longing. The trembling in Johanna's belly ignited into a heat so intense, she could hardly stand. Breaking the kiss, she took Ellie's hand and stepped back, sitting on the nearest bed. She drew Ellie close to stand before her, wrapping her arms around her waist and pressing her cheek to her breast. Ellie's nipples strained at the thin fabric of her nightie, and when Johanna nuzzled them with her lips, Ellie gasped, clutching Johanna's shoulders to steady herself.

Johanna looked up to find Ellie's eyes closed, her bottom lip caught between her teeth. "My God, you're so lovely." She stroked Ellie's breast with her fingers, making her tremble. "I need to see you, Ellie. May I?"

Ellie looked at her, her blue eyes darker and heavy-lidded with desire, and nodded. Johanna leaned down and caught the hem of Ellie's nightgown between her fingers. She raised it slowly, caressing Ellie's skin with the soft material. When she reached the tops of her thighs, Johanna stood and eased the garment up and over Ellie's head.

"Oh, my," she said, drinking in the exquisite sight before her.

Ellie cheeks flamed and she looked away, suddenly shy. The way Johanna looked at her made her skin tingle and her belly tighten almost painfully.

"You are the most beautiful thing I've ever seen," Johanna said, a look of wonder on her face, and her words made Ellie's heart rejoice. Emboldened by desire, she pulled Johanna close, her nipples aching with need as they grazed the cotton of her shift, and kissed her deeply. She ran her hands beneath the fabric to touch the hot skin beneath.

"Off," she said. "I need to feel you." Johanna groaned softly and removed the final barrier between them. They stood, breast to breast, belly to belly, and the intoxicating feel of Johanna's skin on hers made Ellie nearly cry out in pleasure. She nuzzled Johanna's neck, nipping and kissing as her hands roamed the contours of her back and hips. Johanna, breathing heavily, smoothed her hands over the swell of Ellie's bottom. She kissed her softly, then moved away to draw the coverlet down.

"Come lie with me," Johanna said, her voice husky and low.

Ellie's arousal surged at those words, and she stepped forward. Hands on Johanna's shoulders, she pressed her down onto the bed and straddled her hips. Johanna cupped her breasts, circling the taut nipples with her thumbs. Ellie leaned forward, bringing her breasts to Johanna's waiting lips. At the first touch of Johanna's tongue, Ellie's hips surged, coating Johanna's belly with wetness. She moaned at the incredible sensations Johanna was creating as she licked and sucked.

"Oh, I...oh!" She was incoherent with desire, and when Johanna slipped a hand between them and cupped her sex, she cried out.

"You feel like velvet," Johanna marveled. "So soft and wet." Her fingers explored and stroked, the pleasure building until Ellie could bear it no longer. Just when she felt she'd reached the pinnacle of sensation, Johanna entered her, turning the ripples of pleasure into waves that crashed over her body. She thrust hard against Johanna's hand, called out her name as the climax shattered her. Johanna caught Ellie as she collapsed and held her close, stroking her hair until her breathing calmed.

Moving to lie beside her, Ellie looked at her lover in wonder. "My God, I have no words."

Johanna grinned. "Amazing, incredible, fantastic come to mind."

"Yes, yes, all of those and more," Ellie said, nodding emphatically. "Oh, Johanna, I never knew I could feel this way. How can I explain the most wonderful thing that's ever happened to me?"

Johanna put a finger to Ellie's lips. "No words, love. Show me."

And Ellie did. She claimed Johanna's lips, trying to convey all she was feeling through her kisses. When Johanna began to move beneath her, Ellie's lips strayed, and she covered Johanna's skin with kisses on a slow journey to her breasts. When she took a pebbled nipple into her mouth, Johanna groaned and bucked her hips, which excited Ellie even more.

"My body's on fire, lass," Johanna said, as she watched Ellie make love to her breasts. "Touch me."

Ellie, stunned at the effect she was having on Johanna, was enjoying herself immensely. "Is this where you want to be touched?" she said, trailing a finger down Johanna's arm.

"Nae," Johanna said, shaking her head.

Ellie drew slow circles on Johanna's belly. "Here?"

"You're closer."

"Or maybe here," Ellie said, leaning down to run a gentle hand up Johanna's leg from ankle to thigh.

"Christ, woman, don't tease," Johanna said, groaning.

"I want you to feel every bit of the pleasure you gave me," Ellie said, sliding her hand toward Johanna's center. "Tell me what you need."

"You. I need you," Johanna said, taking Ellie's hand and pressing it to her core.

Ellie breath caught as she felt Johanna's arousal and saw it in the flushed skin of her face. "You are so beautiful, my darling," she said. Touching Johanna was heaven, and the enormity of the moment brought tears to her eyes. Johanna's head was tipped back, eyes closed, her dark curls damp on her forehead. Ellie watched Johanna's face as she explored with gentle fingers, witnessing her pleasure with every nuanced change of expression. She caressed Johanna's belly and breasts with her other hand, drawing out the sensations as long as she could.

Johanna whimpered and sighed. "Please, more."

Ellie smiled and shifted to take a nipple in her mouth, while her fingers slowly slid inside. Johanna's hands fisted in the sheets as her hips met Ellie's hand, stroke for stroke. She crested on a long, low moan, capturing Ellie's hand between her trembling thighs, and Ellie's tears spilled as she kissed Johanna's lips.

"My God, that was…och, you're crying. What's the matter, lass?"

"Nothing's the matter. Everything is wonderful. You're breathtaking, Johanna. The sight of you lying here, so beautiful and open and trusting, makes me feel as if I might burst with happiness."

Johanna reached for her, her eyes damp. "Being with you has been the most precious gift. You've made the whole world disappear these few blessed hours and reminded me of what it is to feel joy. Come, dearest, let me hold you."

Ellie wiped her eyes and settled her head on Johanna's shoulder, drawing the covers over them. Johanna held her close, kissing her head and laying her cheek on Ellie's hair. Long after her lover drifted off to sleep, Ellie lay thinking of all that had happened between them since she arrived in France. She wanted this, needed this, and prayed that somehow, it would all work out.

## CHAPTER FOURTEEN

*There were too many. He stood in the road and called to her, and she fought to get to him, tripping over bodies and slipping in the blood-soaked mud. "Duncan! Duncan, wait...I'm coming!" He was yelling something, but she couldn't hear as shells whistled overhead and exploded all around her. She ducked, and when she looked again, he was gone. She ran to where he'd been standing, but all she found was a dead boy with no face. And she screamed.*

The familiar pain crushed Johanna's chest as she bolted upright, bathed in sweat. She looked wildly around in the darkness, yelling out when a hand touched her shoulder.

"Johanna?"

The darkness was suddenly pierced with light, and Johanna found herself in an unfamiliar room. She couldn't stop trembling.

"Johanna, darling, I'm here."

The voice came again, calming her. Warm, gentle hands rubbed her back and smoothed her hair, and she realized where she was. Ellie sat beside her, her face awash with concern.

"Are you all right? You had a bad dream."

Johanna took several deep breaths until she could speak without her voice shaking. "It's always the same." She shuddered.

"Can you talk about it?" Ellie asked.

Johanna scrubbed her hands across her face and sighed. Maybe it was time to face it, this nightmare that had stolen her peace. "There was a boy at the CCS. He came in with several wounded from the Royal Scots—a bullet had grazed his arm. I remembered him especially because he looked very like my brother. He was a friendly lad, and we spoke of home as I tended his arm. He wore a braided leather band around his wrist, a memento from his sweetheart, he said." Johanna wiped her eyes as tears began to fall. "Two weeks later, a wounded soldier grabbed my skirt as I walked by his stretcher. He couldn't speak—his whole jaw was blown away. He had tears in his eyes, and I held his hand as he died. Only then did I notice the leather band on his wrist."

Johanna's tears fell freely now, and Ellie pulled her close, pressing a kiss to her bare shoulder. "I had to cut off his red identification tag for the clerk—it's crazy, but his surname was Duncan." Her voice cracked. "In my dream, the faceless dead boy is my brother. I feel like he is reaching out to me somehow, because I wasn't with him when he died."

"Oh, sweetheart," Ellie said. She gathered Johanna into her arms and held her as she sobbed, purging some of the horrors she had held inside for so long. After a while, her tears stopped, replaced by a desperate need.

"There was so much death in that place, I sometimes felt numb and lifeless myself. And my family, they're all dead, too." She took Ellie's face in her hands and kissed her with urgency. "Touch me, Ellie—I need to feel alive."

Ellie made love to her with all the tenderness and passion she could give, and when the morning came, Johanna knew a part of her had begun to heal.

❖

After two days of kissing and touching freely, the trip back to the hospital was maddening. People were everywhere, and Ellie longed for some privacy. Sighing, she picked up the French newspaper she'd purchased at the station to help pass the time. Johanna was dozing beside her, still not fully rested from her ordeal at the CCS. Ellie felt a twinge low in her belly and smiled, remembering what had kept them from sleeping.

The largest headline spoke of a massive British and French offensive just begun at the Somme. *Ah*, Ellie thought, *that explains all the activity at the station.* A long ambulance train had been on the tracks when they'd arrived in the late afternoon, orderlies filling it with stretchers full of wounded. Nurses rushed to and fro, tending to the men, and a VAD unit had set up a canteen serving cocoa and soup. She and Johanna were traveling back in uniform, and they offered their assistance while waiting for their train. Ellie spent a busy two hours ladling soup into tin bowls and carrying trays of cocoa-filled cups to the soldiers as they waited their turn to board.

When the ambulance train departed, Johanna joined Ellie on the platform. "News from the men isn't good," Johanna said. "They say the first day of the battle was a slaughter." A weary resignation had returned to her eyes, and Ellie was worried that perhaps Johanna needed more time. Even so, there was nothing to be done for it.

"Matron will be wanting us back, then," she replied. "The hospital must be overrun."

Ellie's prediction proved true. The scene was barely controlled chaos when they arrived back at the hospital, and they were pressed into service within minutes of reporting to Matron Campbell. She and Johanna were on different wards and didn't see each other again until well into the next day. She was heading for her hut when she saw Johanna, sitting in one of the folding chairs the convalescents had arranged beneath the canopy of a large tree. Her hands lay still in her lap, her face raised to the sky. Several men sat nearby, playing a raucous game of cards in the shade.

Ellie walked over and gently touched her shoulder. Johanna jumped up, startled, her hand on her chest.

"Och, you nearly scared me to death," Johanna said in mock outrage, but her eyes twinkled.

"I'm so sorry, Jo...I mean, Sister," Ellie said, glancing around. Leaning closer, she whispered, "Are you all right?"

"I am now," Johanna answered, her weary face transformed by her smile. "Rough night."

Ellie nodded. "I was just on my way to take a rest. We're on duty again in four hours. Aren't you going, too?"

"In a minute. I needed some air." Johanna looked into her eyes with an intensity that made her knees weak. "Would you rather rest on the beach?"

Ellie's heart leapt. "Oh yes. Let me wash up, and I'll be along soon."

"I'll be waiting."

Soon after, Johanna was in her arms, her kisses chasing away the darkness. "I missed you," Ellie said. "I didn't like working in the shock ward, away from you."

"I missed you, too, lass. We'll be back to our regular rounds tonight, together in Ward A, thank God," Johanna said. "If I cannot kiss you, at least I want you by my side while we work. You are an exceptional assistant, after all."

"Am I?" Ellie ran her hands slowly up Johanna's chest, then cupped the back of her head and drew her down for a searing kiss. "Do I have any other talents you find exceptional?"

Johanna groaned. "Christ, Ellie, you know the answer to that, and if you kiss me so again, we'll not get any rest."

"Fine," Ellie said, pouting. "Of course you're right, but I don't have to like it."

Johanna laughed. "Did you use that face on your parents to get your way?"

"Oh yes, all the time when I was young. It always worked on my father, but my mother could see right through my schemes," Ellie replied. She took Johanna's hand and led her deeper into their protected hideaway. "I couldn't find a spare blanket this time—we'll have to sit in the sand."

"That's just fine. We're away from the tide line, so our spot is nice and dry." Johanna sat with her back to the cliff wall and pulled Ellie down into her lap. "Here, let me hold you awhile."

Ellie laid her head on Johanna's shoulder and snuggled in. Johanna kissed her forehead and rubbed her back in lazy circles. "I feel so safe with you," Ellie murmured. In moments, she was falling asleep.

"Rest, love," Johanna whispered. "I'm here."

## CHAPTER FIFTEEN

The Somme Offensive raged on as autumn arrived, and the hospital was besieged with badly wounded men, their only blessing the Blighty tickets pinned to their breast pockets that would eventually send them home. Some of those with less serious wounds waited in their hospital blues for the day when the chief medical officer would pass his sentence and send many back to the front. Johanna tried to be reassuring and upbeat for them, knowing how afraid they were, how much they doubted their chances of cheating death twice.

Most of the hospital staff had been working eighteen-hour shifts to handle the scores of wounded coming in each night. Johanna was well past exhausted and felt like an automaton, her humanity slipping away. Her nightmares had abated somewhat, to be replaced by waking hours full of pain and despair. The only thing that was keeping her tethered to hope was Ellie.

Sister Sunshine went about her duties, tenderly ministering to the men, offering a smile, an encouraging word, or a hand to hold whenever she could. Johanna watched this, day after day, and her feelings for Ellie grew ever stronger.

"From what bottomless well do you draw your positive energy?" Johanna asked her one morning over a hurried breakfast in the mess. "You amaze me, you know."

"I don't know," Ellie said. "Maybe it's the stiff upper lip my mother insisted I develop." She rolled her eyes. "I have plenty of low moments, and I've cried myself to sleep more nights than I can count, but as they taught us in VAD training, our role is to ease burdens, not add to them." She sipped her tea, pensive for a moment. "Actually, Sister Lennox, I think you also have a great deal to do with it."

"Me? What do you mean?"

"You have been an inspiration to me from the moment I arrived here. You're strong and compassionate, and you give the same excellent care to each patient, whether he is the first of the day or the hundredth. You are an incredible nurse."

Johanna squirmed in her seat and looked away, uncomfortable with such lavish praise. "Go on, now. I'm nothing special."

Ellie touched her hand with a swift, whisper-soft caress, compelling Johanna to meet her eyes. "Everything about you is special," she said softly.

"Sister Lennox, Miss Winthrop." Johanna jumped at the sound of Matron Campbell's voice, and her face flamed. She'd been staring into the depths of Ellie's soft eyes like a lovesick schoolgirl, and she prayed to all things holy that Matron hadn't noticed.

"Good morning, Matron," Ellie said sweetly, her face the vision of composure.

"Good morning. Miss Winthrop, kindly come to my office when you have finished here."

"Yes, Matron."

Matron Campbell stood there a moment or two longer, eyebrow seemingly raised in question, and Johanna's heart beat faster. Then Matron nodded and walked on. Johanna blew out a breath, worried now.

"What do you think she wants?" Ellie whispered, her face betraying her nervousness.

"I've no idea, but you'd best not keep her waiting. We'll talk later."

Ellie nodded and stood. "Thank you for your time, Sister," she said at her normal volume and left.

As she walked across the grounds to Matron's office, Ellie tried to think what could be the purpose of her summons. She'd only been called to Matron's office one other time since her arrival, and that had led to her working with Johanna. She believed her work was satisfactory, and she and Johanna had been very careful in their personal interactions. The not knowing made her stomach churn uncomfortably, but she walked on. When she arrived at the correct building, she took a deep breath and knocked.

"Come," Matron called.

Ellie entered the spartan little area that Matron used as her office. "You wanted to see me, ma'am?"

"Yes, Miss Winthrop. Please have a seat. I trust things are going well?"

"Yes, Matron, I think so, considering how very busy it's been." Ellie's nerves got the best of her. "Have you heard otherwise, ma'am?" she blurted.

Matron Campbell smiled. "On the contrary, Miss Winthrop. I've received a number of excellent reports about your work. A little birdie told me that the men call you Sister Sunshine."

Ellie's cheeks burned. "I assure you, Matron, I haven't encouraged—"

"At ease, Miss Winthrop. It is a great compliment to be noticed and appreciated by the very ones you are here to serve. I've also heard from the surgeons that you've become quite adept at dressing wounds."

"Thank you, Matron. I've done my best to learn, but the credit should rightfully go to Sister Lennox for her fine and patient tutelage," Ellie replied.

"Quite so," Matron said. "Sister Lennox is an excellent nurse, but she hasn't developed many professional attachments to other staff members. You should feel honored that she has taken you under her wing, so to speak, to advance your skills."

"Oh yes, I am very lucky indeed," Ellie said, the mere mention of Johanna making her light up inside.

"Yes, well," Matron said, clearing her throat. "You have been recommended for the efficiency stripe, a decoration given to those volunteers who have exceeded expectations and provided commendable service." Matron produced an embroidered scarlet stripe, which she proceeded to pin to Ellie's upper sleeve. "Wear this proudly, Miss Winthrop. You've earned it. Congratulations, young lady."

Ellie was relieved and proud in equal measures. "Thank you, Matron. I am honored."

"Go on and get some rest. I expect we'll have another influx tonight. You are dismissed, Miss Winthrop."

Ellie nodded and took her leave. Her attempts to find Johanna were unsuccessful, so she assumed she'd gone to her quarters, a place where Ellie most definitely could not be seen. Her news would have to wait until their shift began. Ellie touched the stripe on her sleeve and smiled, then headed off to her hut for some much-needed sleep.

❖

"Might I have a word, Sister Lennox?"

Johanna looked up from the bowl in which she was preparing carbolic lotion to find Matron Campbell in the doorway of the dispensary.

"Of course, Matron."

"I've been remiss in not thanking you for the training you've done with the volunteers. I know you were not keen on working with them a few months ago."

Johanna shrugged with a smile. "Turned out I was worried for naught. They're a good bunch."

"Indeed. You are aware that Miss Winthrop earned her efficiency stripe?"

"Aye, and I'm glad for her—she works very hard and is a quick learner," Johanna replied.

"She gave much of the credit to you, as it happens," Matron said.

"Did she?" Johanna hoped the meager light would hide the fire in her cheeks.

Matron nodded. "I've noticed that you have made her into a protégé of sorts, and that you seem quite fond of each other."

Johanna sucked in a breath. *Oh, bloody hell.* She tried for a look of indifference, and since she had no idea what to say, she simply nodded.

"Knowing your tendency to avoid unnecessary interactions, I must say I'm surprised at the interest you've taken in the young lady."

Johanna's stomach felt as if she'd swallowed lead, but she found her voice and fought mightily to keep it calm. "As I said, she's a hard worker and a great help on the ward. She's smart and wants to learn. Is it wrong of me to assist in her professional growth?"

"Not at all, but you mustn't give the appearance of favoritism. Miss Winthrop clearly idolizes you, but she's young and inexperienced in the ways of the world. We wouldn't want there to be any suspicion of impropriety."

Impropriety? "Has someone complained? Have the other volunteers said I haven't trained them properly?" Oh, Christ, did she know?

"No one has said anything directly to me, but if I am noticing such things, perhaps others are as well. Listen, Johanna," Matron lowered her voice, "you are one of my best nurses. I'm just looking out for you, lass."

"Thank you, Matron, but you have nothing to worry about," Johanna said, the lie burning like acid on her tongue.

## CHAPTER SIXTEEN

D o you think she knows?" Ellie said, shivering in her mackintosh. They had stolen a few moments down on the beach, but the exhausting pace of work and the cold, rainy weather had made those moments difficult to find.

"She knows we're fond of each other, but Matron was warning me not to give the appearance of favoritism," Johanna replied.

"Oh," Ellie said, remembering, "maybe that's what the girls meant when they said I had your ear."

"What?"

"Mary and Daisy were telling secrets in our hut one night when I was pretending to be asleep. They thought if I overheard, I'd go right off to tell you, since I had your ear. Ugh, I'm sorry I didn't realize before."

"Maybe it wouldn't have been as obvious if I wasn't so bloody standoffish. You're the only volunteer who isn't afraid of me." Johanna looked hurt, and Ellie squeezed her hand, laughing.

"Well, you are tall, dark, and brooding. The first time I saw you, two things struck me at once—you were very beautiful, and very stern."

"Well, I don't know about beautiful, but I was going for stern that day. I thought if Matron was putting me in charge of your lot, I'd better establish my authority. Generally, though, I don't mean to be so unapproachable. I'm just not very good at small talk and such."

"I know, darling. You don't have to be a social butterfly, but a smile goes a long way. It was your smile that first gave me a glimpse of the wonderful person you are, underneath that stern exterior." Ellie leaned in and gave Johanna a gentle kiss. "But don't go smiling too much at the other girls. I rather like being the only one who has your ear," she teased, giving Johanna's earlobe a tug with her teeth, "and your neck, and your..."

Johanna silenced her with a long, deep kiss. "How am I supposed to pretend you're not my favorite when you say such things?" She touched her forehead to Ellie's and sighed. "It's hard to pretend, but we must. Matron was kind to warn me, but we can't afford to give anyone else ideas."

"Agreed." Ellie gave her a hug and stepped back. "You'd better go on back, then. I'll be along shortly."

She watched Johanna walk away, fully aware of the risks Johanna was taking for her. Her fear of discovery was why she had run away to the CCS in the first place. Now that their relationship had become intimate, the risks were even greater. Ellie hated that they had no privacy to express their feelings physically, or to have anything beyond cursory conversations, but she had to make sure no one else suspected. She had to protect Johanna.

❖

Ellie came up with a plan to defy their circumstances. She'd found a suitable crack behind a shelf in the dispensary, which was deep enough to hold a slip of paper but could not be seen if one wasn't looking. That night, at the end of their shift, she slipped a note into Johanna's apron pocket explaining her idea. She felt silly as a schoolgirl passing notes in class, but it was the only way she could speak plainly.

At the start of the next day's shift, Ellie feared Johanna disapproved of her plan. Johanna had looked at her with a scowl on her face, but after glancing around to make sure no one was looking, she'd winked with a smile and inclined her head toward the dispensary. Ellie checked her hiding spot as soon as she could.

"What's your favorite color?" she had asked.

*The lovely blue of your eyes. What is your most favorite food?*

Ellie scribbled her answer and another question and tucked the note away. And so it went on for the next three weeks. They were getting to know each other on paper, but the questions and answers became bolder.

*What do you think of before you fall asleep?* she asked.

And Johanna replied, *Tasting your lips and touching your beautiful body. I wish we could go to the beach. Damn this miserable weather!*

The blustery days had greatly outnumbered the sunny ones in the past month, and Ellie longed for the summer's warmth as she layered long underwear beneath her uniform. It had taken forever to get even a little warm earlier, and an irritating cough had taken up residence in her chest. Sleep had eluded her, despite her exhaustion. She donned her mac and headed for Ward A, turning her face from the driving rain. Why did it seem as if the ward had moved farther away? Ellie trudged on and was thoroughly damp when she arrived. Warming her hands by the little brazier that struggled to heat the place, she looked about for Johanna.

She saw her at the far end, changing the bandage on an amputee's stump, and as she headed there to help, a coughing fit overtook her. How odd she felt all of a sudden! Everything seemed muted, as if she was looking through a haze, and she could barely hear over the pounding in her head. She grabbed blindly for something to steady her. The last thing she saw was Johanna's worried face before everything went black.

❖

Johanna had been looking forward to seeing Ellie all day. Their last note had her body thrumming with pent-up desire, and she needed to be near her. She glanced up from the dressing she was changing when Ellie entered the ward. Smiling to herself, she brought her focus back to the young private who had lost his leg, finishing her work. She patted his shoulder and, hearing a spate of coughing, looked up in time to see Ellie swaying on her feet. She was white as a sheet.

"Ellie!" Johanna rushed to catch her as she fainted. Sister Longley came to help, and they laid her down on the only empty cot in the ward.

"She's burning up," Sister Longley said. "Must be pneumonia—Ward D is overflowing with cases."

"Here, let's put the screen up around her—I don't want to move her to the sisters' infirmary in this rain. Can you grab extra pillows? She must be propped up. We need to sponge her with alcohol. Ellie, can you hear me?" Johanna, usually the picture of calm in a crisis, was beside herself with worry.

Sister Longley sent one of the VAD girls to fetch Matron Campbell, then helped Johanna remove Ellie's uniform. Over the next three hours, they attempted to lower Ellie's temperature with alcohol baths and a salt-solution enema, applied a mustard plaster to her chest, and spoon-fed her a mixture of milk and whiskey every hour. Throughout their ministrations, Ellie could only moan, delirious and racked by coughing fits.

As soon as the rain abated, they moved her to the infirmary that housed the sick and injured female staff. Johanna reluctantly left her in the care of others and went back to finish her work in Ward A.

"Sister Sunshine's taken ill, then?" a corporal said as she checked his shoulder wound for infection.

"Aye," Johanna nodded, barely able to speak.

"A right shame, that," he said. "Never met a sweeter lass."

Johanna suppressed a sob as she replaced his bandage, then stepped into the dispensary for a moment's privacy. Ellie was in danger, and Johanna was sick with worry. She'd seen many men die of the same affliction, their fluid-filled lungs drowning them. She couldn't bear the thought of Ellie…No, it would be all right. Ellie was strong, and Johanna would do everything in her power to keep her alive.

"Sister Lennox." The faint voice grew stronger, and Johanna opened her eyes to find Matron Campbell leaning over her.

"What is it?" she said, jumping up. "Ellie…"

"She's still with us, in no small part thanks to you. But, Johanna, you must go rest in your quarters. You're at high risk to contract the illness yourself, and you won't be any good to anyone if you get sick."

"I'm fine, Matron. I can't leave her until she's out of danger."

"You're a bloody hardheaded Scot, and being one myself, I can say so. I'll not force you to go just yet...It's plain to see that Miss Winthrop is very dear to you. However, I must remind you that your duty is to the wounded, and I need you at your post, rested and able to handle what comes. Have I made myself clear, Sister?"

"Yes, Matron. You're a kind woman, and I thank you for understanding." Johanna looked over at the bed where Ellie lay, so fragile and pale. "She has become like family to me, what with my own people gone," she said, her voice trembling. "I couldn't do a thing to help them in their hour of need, but I must try for Ellie."

Matron Campbell laid a hand on Johanna's shoulder. "You've done all you can, my dear. The rest is in the hands of God."

After Matron had gone, Johanna went to Ellie's side. She rubbed camphorated oil on her chest and throat to ease her labored and shallow breathing, praying that what they had done for the last four days would be enough. As tears slid down her face, she leaned close to Ellie's ear. "Keep fighting, my darling. I love you."

❖

Johanna had just finished her rounds with the surgeon when Sister Longley rushed in. "Her fever has broken, thank the heavens, and she's asking for you."

The surge of relief nearly brought Johanna to her knees. Sister Longley grasped her arm. "Steady on, Sister Lennox. I'll stay here—you go."

"Thank you," Johanna said, tears filling her eyes. "Thank you for everything."

Johanna ran to the infirmary, mindless of the cold and mud. When she arrived, Matron and another nurse were bent over the bed, obscuring her view of Ellie. She rushed forward to find Ellie sitting up, taking spoonfuls of soup. She was still pale, but despite the dark smudges beneath them, her blue eyes were clear and bright. Her gown was askew, her hair a mess, and she'd never looked more beautiful.

"Johanna," she said, her voice barely a whisper. Ellie smiled, but it faded as she must have remembered her audience. "Um, hello, Sister Lennox."

Matron Campbell cleared her throat. "Never mind that, child. This woman spent every minute she could by your side for days. I think we can dispense with the formalities."

Johanna shot her a grateful look, and Matron nodded. "Come, Sister Ryan. I think we are needed elsewhere just now."

When the other women left, Johanna knelt by Ellie's bed and took her hand. "How are you feeling?"

Ellie groaned. "Like I went through a washerwoman's wringer. I can barely move."

"Aye, but you look a good deal better than you have lately. My God, Ellie, I was so worried."

"So I gathered. You spent your off-duty time here?"

"I did, whenever I could. They tried to shoo me away, but I wouldn't go." Johanna squeezed Ellie's hand. "I just couldn't leave you."

"I thought I'd dreamed it," Ellie said, her eyes filling with tears. "I was aware of people around me, but in my dream, a lovely dark-haired angel came. She had a soothing voice and gentle hands, and she...she told me she loved me."

"It wasn't a dream, lass. I'm no angel, but I do love you so."

Ellie's chest heaved with great, aching sobs that had her gasping for air.

"Nae, Ellie, don't cry. You must calm down so you can breathe." Johanna stroked Ellie's arm. "That was not the reaction I'd hoped for when I said those words," she said, trying for levity.

"Oh, Johanna, what will we do?" The despair on Ellie's face tore at Johanna's heart.

"What do you mean?"

"The doctor was here before. He said I cannot work, that I must have a long rest. Johanna, my darling, I love you, too, but they're sending me back to England."

Johanna's heart sank as the implications of this news hit home. Of course Ellie was leaving—she'd nearly died, and her lungs needed time to heal. But Johanna was here for the duration, however long that would be. They'd found each other here in the harsh reality of war, somehow out of time, out of place, but Ellie was going back to the real world, to England, to her home. How could their love possibly survive now?

## CHAPTER SEVENTEEN

*Three weeks later*

The place that had been home for Ellie's entire life now felt oddly foreign. The house itself was familiar, its gray stone exterior and tall windows solid and reassuring, unlike so many of its French counterparts which now lay in ruins. It was still full of familiar things—brocade chairs and high-backed chesterfields, mahogany sideboards and gilded tables, the same vases on the same pedestals in the same parlor where a telegram had redirected the course of her life. Yes, everything was familiar, but she, Eleanor Winthrop, had fundamentally changed.

She'd been back just a few days, after spending nearly two weeks in a women's convalescent camp before they'd allowed her to board the ship home. Unable to do much but sit about, she'd begun writing to Johanna. She had no one else with whom she could share her feelings, and she'd never felt so lonely.

*My Dearest Johanna,*

*I'm home now five days, and the inactivity is maddening. I miss you terribly! The convalescent camp was necessary, I suppose, to help me gain strength, but the sister in charge of my* care was a bit too heavy-handed for my liking. How I longed for your gentle touch, my darling! My mother hovers over me constantly, as if I might keel over and die at any moment. She doesn't like that I escape to my room whenever possible, but the last thing I want is to be sociable. I cannot speak of my experiences in France to anyone here—they could never understand.

I have heard that Theo is somewhere near Saint-Omer and has managed to stay alive. My worry for him is overwhelming, having seen what we've seen. The two of you are nearly all I can think about, and I hate being here, helpless and weak. How selfish of me to say that, as I rest here in peace while you remain in hell. Still, I would gladly trade my comforts to be with you, my love. I pray every day for your safety and for an end to this war. I grieve for the countless souls who have died, but I can't help feeling grateful, for without the war, I would never have met you.

I've sent along some things that I hope will bring you comfort—please share them with the other sisters with thanks for saving my life. Such small tokens will never repay you all, and I wish I could deliver them myself. When I close my eyes, I think of your arms holding me, and of your sweet kisses. I must survive on my dreams until the day we meet again. Please, God, let it be soon. Write to me.

With love,
Ellie

❖

Johanna trudged through the days, melancholy weighing her down. Though Ellie had come through the worst of her illness, she'd still been so weak, and not knowing how she was doing now was driving Johanna mad with worry. She'd promised she would write when she got back home, and Johanna had awaited mail call each day, only to have her hopes dashed when no letters arrived. Sick of her heart jerking up and down like a bandalore, she stopped checking.

As she settled onto her cot after another long night shift, Sister Longley burst into their shared quarters. "Look, it's a parcel from Ellie Winthrop," she said, holding a box wrapped in brown paper. "Matron asked me to fetch it when I went to mail a letter. Must be she made it home all right, poor girl. How I wish I could be back in England again."

Johanna barely heard a word beyond *Ellie Winthrop* as she jumped up and took the package. Sister Longley was hovering, no doubt excited to see what the box contained, but Johanna suddenly wanted her privacy.

"Thank you for bringing it over. I reckon I'll open it after I've had a bit of sleep." Johanna tucked the box under her cot and slid back beneath the covers, feigning exhaustion with a yawn.

"Oh. Well, then, do tell us how she's getting on, won't you?" Johanna felt a twinge of guilt at the disappointment in Sister Longley's voice, but she wanted to be alone when she opened the parcel.

After several agonizing minutes of waiting with her eyes shut while Longley puttered around, Johanna finally heard her leave. She snatched up the box, gazing at Ellie's familiar script on the paper. Taking care to save the return address, she tore away the paper and string to find a box, gift-wrapped in lovely paper printed with holly and bows and bound with a red ribbon. She'd forgotten that it was very near Christmastime—it was so easy to lose track of days here. She untied the ribbon, carefully removed the gift wrap, and opened the box, her heart thudding in her chest.

On top lay an envelope addressed to Sister Lennox, and Johanna smiled at Ellie's attempts to keep up appearances even now. Putting the letter aside, she removed item after item from the box, delighting in her treasures. There was a pair of thick woolen socks, two bars of lavender soap, a volume of Emily Dickinson's poetry, a box of chocolates, several tins of hand lotion, rose-colored stationery, a pen and felt-wrapped bottle of ink, and a packet of shortbread biscuits.

Johanna lifted the soap to her nose, the heady scent causing a surge of heat in her depths as she thought of the hotel in Paris, and how Ellie had smelled, warm and fragrant from her bath. She closed her eyes and breathed it in, remembering. After several long moments, she picked up the envelope and withdrew the letter inside. Tears flowed unchecked as she read Ellie's words of love. She seemed worlds away, and Johanna ached inside. Wiping her eyes, she took up the pen, needing to connect with Ellie in the only way she could.

*My Dearest Ellie,*

*I've missed you so, and receiving your letter and gifts breathed a new life into me. I am so grateful that you are safe at home, away from this place, even though your absence for me is like a wound that won't heal. I, too, pray every day for an end to this madness. Before you, I didn't much care how long the war carried on, having nothing and no one to go home to. Now, the war is far crueler for keeping me from you.*

*I will share the chocolates and lotions with the other sisters, and I'm sure they'll be happy to hear of your improved health.*

*You'll be glad to know that I've made friends among them. They were so kind to me when you were ill. No one seemed to question my devotion to you, and that has earned them my gratitude.*

*Good news about your brother—I will add my prayers to yours for his safety. Things here have slowed down a bit. We're receiving many more cases of frostbite, trench fever, and pneumonia than wounded, just now, though the outcome is often just as grim. Four new volunteers arrived a fortnight past, and guess who was sent to meet them? I will never forget my first glimpse of you at the station, all fresh-faced and determined, and so beautiful. I didn't know I could find a woman so beguiling, and I think I must have fallen for you a wee bit that day. You are the best thing in my life, darling Ellie, and I beg God to make our time apart pass swiftly.*

*I will sleep with the lavender soap in my pillow and dream every night of holding you and loving you. Please keep writing— your letters will be my lifeblood until I see you again. For now, I'll send my kisses on the wind.*

*Yours,*

*Johanna*

## CHAPTER EIGHTEEN

*April 1917*

"We'll bloody well beat the Boche now, lads!" Similar cries rose from the crowd of walking wounded that had gathered outside the ward.

Johanna stopped one of the VADs. "What are they going on about out there?"

"I'll find out, Sister," the volunteer said. A few moments later, she rushed back in, a huge smile on her face. "The Americans have agreed to join the fight! The men feel sure this will turn the tide. Isn't it wonderful news?"

"Aye, it is," she said. With the help of the Americans, perhaps the war truly could be near its end. But why did such exciting news fill her with trepidation? This place had become her life, had seeped into every crevice of her heart and soul. Here, she had a purpose and knew what was expected of her. She was not the same person who had left Scotland a few short years ago. She wanted nothing more than to see Ellie again, but who would they be together without the war to bind them? Her intense longing for Ellie battled with a niggling worry that kept intruding into her mind, growing stronger as the days passed. *You will never truly belong with a woman like Ellie.*

She shook her head and went about her duties, willing her mind to focus on the here and now. Right now, these men needed her, and in some strange way, she needed them, too.

"Pardon me, Sister?"

Johanna turned to the speaker and gasped. A tall young lieutenant stood there, cap in his uninjured hand. His reddish-blond hair and bright blue eyes reminded her so much of Ellie, it hurt to look at him.

"Yes, Lieutenant?"

"I was wondering if you could help me. I've only just arrived, but I think this may be the hospital my sister spoke of. She is with a Voluntary Aid Detachment, you see, and she wrote that she was stationed in Boulogne. Perhaps you know of her?"

Johanna's eyes flew to his identification tag. *T. Winthrop.* Oh, Christ. "Theo?"

The young man's eyes widened. "Why, yes, that's my name. How..."

"Your sister is Eleanor Winthrop?"

"Yes! My God, is she here?"

Johanna's heart lurched. "She was. Came down with pneumonia and was sent home, a month ago. She spoke of you often—thank God you're all right."

The young man's face fell. "I had so hoped to see her, but that's jolly good news she's gone home." He held up his bandaged hand. "Lost a couple of fingers, but I can still fire my weapon and drive, so I imagine I'll be back with my men very soon. Did you know my sister well?"

Johanna swallowed, fighting back tears. "Aye, Ellie is a dear friend, and she was a favorite among the men. Sister Sunshine, they called her." Her throat ached with emotion. "We miss her very much."

"Ah, that's Ellie, a friend to everyone. Every chap in town wanted to marry her, but she always put them off, the poor fellows."

The thought of Ellie marrying made Johanna's blood run cold, but she hid her discomfort with a smile. "She was my assistant of sorts here and became quite skilled. What regiment are you with, Lieutenant?"

"We're with the Fourth London Field Ambulance, Transport Unit. And please, call me Theo. Any friend of Ellie's is a friend of mine."

Johanna liked him instantly. "Right, Theo. I'm Sister Lennox—Johanna. How did you get injured?"

"Bloody shell exploded by the supply wagon we were loading. The wagon took the brunt, but we lost one man and a horse besides. Everyone there was wounded—I was damned lucky, I'll tell you, if you'll pardon my tongue." He blushed and ducked his head. "Sorry, ma'am. Got into some bad habits here without my mother censoring my language every five minutes."

"You're not offending me. I've heard and said worse." Johanna looked at his dirty, blood-stained field dressing. "No one's tended to you yet?"

"I'm all right. Just been checking to see that my men are taken care of first."

The way he cradled his hand and the strain of discomfort on his face told Johanna a different story. "That dressing needs to be changed. Since you're here, and I've just finished my rounds, I'll see to it. Come, sit." Johanna pointed Theo to a chair and fetched the supply cart.

Theo winced when she began removing the dressing but said nothing. Johanna peeled the bandages away to find his ring and little fingers gone, a ragged hole in their place. The knucklebones stood out white amidst the blackened and bloody flesh, and a greenish pus oozed from the wound.

Johanna swore under her breath. "When did this happen?"

"Three days ago. The others are wounded far worse than I. They were a much higher priority."

"That was very gallant of you, Theo, but if we don't get this cleaned up quickly, you're going to lose this hand."

Theo blanched and swallowed hard. "I understand," he said.

Johanna grabbed a basin and went to fill it with saline. She washed and rinsed his wound repeatedly, distracting him with talk of home. "Tell me about your house." She listened as he painted a picture with his words, of a sprawling manor on a hundred acres of woods and cultivated fields, pastures, and streams.

"It sounds like a wonderful place. I can picture you and Ellie there."

Theo sucked in a breath, sweat beading on his forehead. "Could you stop for a moment, Sister?"

"I know it's painful, Theo," Johanna said, rubbing his arm. "I'm nearly done, and then I'll bandage you up until the surgeon can see you. Tell me where you would be if you were home right now."

Theo closed his eyes. "I'd be at the stables, likely as not. Horses are my great love, and William, our stable master, was like a second father to me growing up. With the horses is where I find my peace." As Johanna began bandaging his hand, Theo chuckled. "After a long ride on Samson, I'd often torment Cook by sneaking into the kitchen and stealing sweets. She'd fuss, but I think she made extra just for me." His voice had taken on a melancholy timbre, and Johanna glanced up to find tears in the young man's eyes.

"I took it for granted before all this," he said, looking around the ward. "I hope someday to see my home again, but if I don't, at least I know Ellie is safe now."

Johanna, fighting her own tears, clasped his good hand. "You'll see her again. God willing, we both will."

❖

The surgeon was able to save Theo's hand, thanks in no small part to Johanna's intervention. Since he was an officer and could move about freely, Theo took to meeting her for breakfast in the mess after her shift. They became fast friends, and Johanna felt a stronger connection to Ellie with him there.

He was very like his sister—friendly, easygoing, and respectful of everyone, regardless of rank or station. Unlike some officers who conducted themselves with an air of superiority and aloofness, Theo interacted comfortably with his men, and they in turn held him in high esteem.

"Is it true about the Americans, then?" Johanna asked one morning, after a particularly difficult shift.

"Yes, Wilson finally declared war on Germany after they'd sunk too many ships for him to ignore. About bloody time, I say."

"How long before they arrive, do you think?"

"They'll need to muster, train, and mobilize an entire army. Don't imagine we'll get much help until late summer. We'll just need to hold 'em back a bit longer."

"My God, it seems we barely have an army left. I couldn't count the number of dead and wounded I've seen, and we're but one hospital of many." Johanna shook her head. "It's all been so overwhelming."

Theo reached out and patted her arm. "There would be a great deal more dead were it not for you and your fellow nurses. I, for one, am deeply grateful for your service."

Johanna's heart swelled. Theo was a good man, one she'd fancy marrying if she wasn't already in love with his sister. Just as quickly as that thought crossed her mind, the insidious voice of doubt crept in. *Know your place. You'll never be one of them.*

"Thank you, Theo," she said, rising from her chair. He stood quickly, ever the gentleman. "I need to rest now. See you tomorrow?"

"I'll be here."

She nodded and hurried off to her quarters, where she could hide under her blankets and cry in private. She missed Ellie so much it hurt to breathe.

## CHAPTER NINETEEN

W
e've each got a letter from Theo," Mother said, her face awash with happiness and relief.

"Oh, Theo, thank goodness."

Mother began to open her letter, then said, "Oh, you've got another one, too." Ellie forced herself to remain calm, though she wanted to shout for joy when she recognized Johanna's handwriting on the other envelope. She opened Theo's first.

*Dear Sis,*

*You'll never guess where I am. I went and got my hand wounded, and they brought me to your hospital in Boulogne. I was very sorry I couldn't see you, but I'm thrilled you made it back home. Your nurse friend Johanna took brilliant care of me, and the surgeon fixed me up fine. I'm two fingers short of a full hand now, but that's war. Johanna is ace—I can see why you became friends. We spend our breakfast time together every morning now, and talk about you often. She's quite fond of you, Sis, and I do hope we can all meet up when this blasted war is good and done. Maybe when the Americans get here, we can finally send those Huns back where they belong.*

*I don't suppose I'll be getting my Blighty ticket yet. I can still do my job, but the MO will have the final word. They're so desperate for men at the front, I say he won't be too keen on letting me go. Thank God I had the sense to avoid infantry duty. At least I don't have to live up to my knees in muck like those poor blokes in the trenches.*

*Tell Mother and Father not to worry. I'm enjoying my work and happy to be doing my bit for Britain. I've got a fine group of men in my unit, and they all treat me with respect, even the old codgers. I'll probably be here another week or two, so write back.*

*Until then, I remain your most wonderful brother,*
*Theo*

Ellie wiped her eyes, grinning at her brother's cheek. She couldn't get over the fact that he was there with Johanna—what great good luck!

"What is an MO?" Mother asked. Theo had evidently shared that information in her letter as well.

"Medical Officer. They evaluate the patients and decide who must go home and who is fit to stay in the fight."

"Well, surely this medical officer will release your brother from duty. For heaven's sake, he's wounded."

Ellie sighed. There were just some things Mother would never understand. "It isn't likely. I've helped patch up men with worse wounds, only to see them sent back to their regiments. It's a nasty business, you know."

Mother huffed. "Well, perhaps I *would* know if you ever spoke to me about it."

"I don't care to talk about it. Trust me, Mother—in this case, ignorance is bliss. I'm going up to my room for a rest."

"Fine, then. Don't be late for dinner."

Ellie snatched up her letters and left, needing to be away from her mother's badgering. It hadn't taken her long to expect Ellie to pick up right where she'd left off before, as if the last ten months had never happened.

Back in her room, she put her mother out of her head and focused on Johanna's letter. She brought the envelope to her nose, imagining Johanna's scent, then ran her finger over the neat black script, savoring every detail. Fetching her letter opener from the bedside table drawer, she freed Johanna's words into her eager hands.

*My Darling,*

*Theo is here! He walked right into the ward and asked if I knew of his sister—I nearly fell over from the shock. He's a braw young lad, and kind. He looks so much like you, and I miss you even more, if that's possible. Don't fash about his wound— he was lucky and will be just fine. I don't reckon we'll be able to keep him much longer, and I'll be very sad to see him go.*

*Now that spring is here, I go to our spot on the beach whenever I can get away. It's where I feel closest to you, my love, but sometimes I want to hold you so badly I can't bear it. Theo told me all about your home, and I can imagine you there, strolling about the gardens or reading a book, surrounded by pretty things that are no match for your beauty. There I go, fancying myself a poet. I'm so grateful for the poems you sent—I read them every day, and they sustain me.*

*I hope you are well and recovering quickly, darling. I'm holding up all right, but I'd give anything for a repeat of our time in Paris. My lavender-scented pillow takes me to you in my dreams. I pray the Americans can give our side the strength it needs to end this nightmare once and for all, for the sooner it's over, the sooner I can see you again. I'll step outside now to send more kisses on the wind.*

    *Love,*

    *Johanna*

Ellie lay on the bed, clutching the letter to her chest, and cried.

❖

Johanna stood in the rain as the orderlies loaded the wounded into the ambulances. Most were headed to the port and the waiting hospital ship bound for England, but a few, like Theo, were going back to the war. She watched him clasp the hand of a soldier on a stretcher, knowing he was bidding farewell to one of his men. She'd seen such moments a hundred times, but this one touched her in a different way. She'd come to care for Theo, and she would be praying for his safety once again.

"Cheer up, Johanna," he said, coming to stand before her. "It can't rain forever."

"I don't care a lick about the weather, Lieutenant, and you know it."

Theo laughed. "Well, if we've gone back to formalities, then…" He took Johanna's hand and kissed it. "I'm honored to have met you, Sister Lennox. And if I may be so bold, I feel as if I've gained a friend in you. We'll meet again, I feel sure of it." He smiled, and on impulse, Johanna reached up to kiss his cheek.

"Be safe, then, lad. You need to get back to stealing the bacon off Ellie's plate." She smiled back at him, trying to hold her tears at bay.

"Ah, Ellie told tales about me, I see. Take care of yourself, Johanna."

"You, too, Theo." She watched him jump into the cab of the ambulance and waved as they drove away.

*Protect him, sweet Jesus, please protect him.*

## CHAPTER TWENTY

Johanna began to measure time by Ellie's letters, which arrived like clockwork once a week. She read and reread them to maintain her sanity, as summer weather meant more frequent battles and more wounded pouring in. She was hot, tired, and sore all the time, but when she received a letter, her discomfort faded.

*My Dearest,*

*I hope it is cooler there than it has been here lately. When it's miserably hot and I can't sleep, I imagine being on our beach with you and wading in the cool water. I try to guess how busy it must be at the hospital by reading the newspapers, but of course they don't tell us the whole truth about battles and such.*

*Here it is a craziness of a different sort. The socialites have decided that the London season must go on, despite those trifling inconveniences of war and rationing. My mother is driving me mad by insisting that I attend this luncheon and that party. I've gone several times just to placate her, but I've found them more boring than ever. Mother has doubled her efforts to marry me off now that I'm home, and she's invited four different men to come calling. I'm running out of excuses to decline them, and it all makes me want to scream. The last one was at least twenty years my senior and smelled like old cheese. Even my father is encouraging me to settle down with someone, the traitor. How I wish you were here to take me away!*

Johanna's chest tightened painfully. How in the world could she take Ellie away from her family, from the only life she'd ever known? She knew how difficult it would be for Ellie to go against her parents' wishes, but if she did, would they disown her? Theo had described their splendid home—Johanna had never set foot in such a place. The best she could hope for would be to find a small flat of her own after the war. Ellie would never be happy giving up her life of wealth and comfort for that.

As these thoughts raced through her mind, Johanna's despair grew. Was she a fool to think there could ever be a happily ever after for her and Ellie? Maybe she was just being selfish. She knew Ellie cared for her, but she was a beautiful, vibrant young woman. She should be with someone who could give her the best in life, and raise children who would want for nothing.

*If I hadn't been so damned weak, I could have avoided all of this, and Ellie would be moving on with her life. Who knows when we might see each other again? I have no right to make her wait.*

Johanna's heart broke as she agonized over her decision, but in the end, she knew what she had to do.

❖

Ellie rushed to her room with the latest letter from Johanna and flopped down, breathless, on her bed. The slight breeze that stirred the curtains at the window did little to cool the air on this hot July afternoon, but it was preferable to sitting in the parlor with Mother and her pretentious friends. Ellie opened the envelope and began to read. Moments later, it was as if the sun had been snuffed out, the air sucked from the room. *No, no, no, no.* Tears sprang to Ellie's eyes as she read the excruciating words.

*Dearest Ellie,*

*Forgive me for what I must do. The moments we spent together were the best of my life, and I will cherish them always. You awakened a part of me, buried deep beneath my pain, that I thought was dead, and I am truly grateful. What we had was the most beautiful dream, my darling, but now that you're gone, the dream is over. You are where you belong and must live the life you were born to live. I cannot share such a life with you—I am only the daughter of a fisherman. God knows when I will ever make it home, but if I do, my work will barely earn a living wage. I could never provide for you all that you deserve, and your parents would surely not accept me. Please know that I do this because I love you. Your happiness is all I hope for, and I can rest easy believing that someday, someone better than me will take care of you. Do not be sad, sweet Ellie—this is for the best. Please, let me go.*

*Johanna*

"Ugh, you foolish, foolish woman!" Ellie pounded the bed with her fists as hot tears spilled from her eyes. She had never experienced such intense pain and suddenly understood what it meant to have a broken heart. She sobbed until no more tears would come, and then, her sadness shifted to anger. Johanna had no right to decide what was best for her, and her stubborn insistence that she wasn't good enough drove Ellie mad with frustration. She could not, would not accept this. Moving to her writing desk, she snatched up her pen and a sheet of stationery. Dipping her pen into the inkwell, she began to write, dribbling ink in her haste to put her thoughts to paper. Johanna Lennox would soon find out that Ellie Winthrop could not be chased away.

❖

Once Johanna had posted her good-bye letter to Ellie, she was again overcome with grief for all she had lost. She believed she had done the right thing, but that was little consolation to her broken heart. She threw herself into her work, seeking the numbness of complete exhaustion. The volunteers and nurses gave her a wide berth, speaking only when necessary. She knew she was allowing her emotions to affect her work and wasn't surprised when Matron Campbell intervened.

"Sister Lennox, a moment, please." She disappeared through the door and Johanna followed. Once outside, Matron Campbell took Johanna's arm and pulled her out of earshot of any passersby. "What is going on with you?"

"I don't want to talk about it," Johanna said, staring at her shoes.

"Humph. You'd bloody well talk about it. The volunteers are afraid to speak to you, the other sisters have had enough of your moodiness, and the patients deserve better."

"I'm sorry, Matron. I've just been upset lately."

"Clearly." Matron lowered her voice and asked, "Does this have anything to do with Ellie Winthrop?"

Johanna jerked her head up, shocked at the question. "What?"

"You know, I'm not blind, Johanna."

"I don't know what you're talking about." Johanna's face burned as her stomach clenched painfully.

"Don't you?" Matron sighed. "After your shift, please come to my office. We need to talk."

Johanna knocked on the door a while later, her thoughts in turmoil. Whatever Matron thought she knew...

"Johanna, please shut the door and come sit."

Johanna sat, feeling more anxious than a naughty pupil in the headmaster's office. Matron Campbell regarded her in silence for a moment, then reached into her desk drawer. "I think this calls for a little taste of home." She pulled out a bottle of Scotch and a couple of small glasses, then poured them each a dram of the amber liquid. Matron took a sip, then said, "I know what you're going through, Johanna, and I've decided to share with you a personal story. No one here knows what I'm about to tell you, but I believe I can trust your discretion."

"Aye, Matron. I'll not breathe a word to anyone."

Matron nodded. "Before the war, I shared my home in London with...a friend. She was a teacher at a primary school. Neither of us had ever wed, and we had what was called a Boston marriage. People likely assumed we were just good friends sharing expenses, but it was more than that. Do you understand what I'm saying?"

Johanna could only nod, unable to believe what she was hearing. This woman, whom she had long admired and respected, carried her own secret.

"I was in love with her, and she with me. We had ten wonderful years together before my Lucy passed, and a large piece of my heart died with her. I know what you and Ellie mean to each other, lass—I suspected for a while, but I knew for sure that you were in love with her when she became ill. One doesn't see such devotion every day, you know."

Johanna took a long sip of Scotch, hoping the burn would rid her throat of the lump that had formed there. Her burden of guilt weighed heavily on her, and she couldn't hold it in any longer.

"Och, Matron, I'm so ashamed," Johanna said, her face burning as she stared into her glass.

"Whatever for?"

"I've behaved unprofessionally. I was irresponsible to let things develop with Ellie, and by God, I tried not to, but—"

"Stop, Johanna. I didn't call you here to chastise you, nor will I allow you to punish yourself. Life is full of the unexpected, and we never know when love will find us. You may have broken the rules, lass, but don't you ever be ashamed of loving her. I know it's been difficult for you since she went home, but there's nothing to be done for it now. We must complete our duty. If you are meant to find her again, you will."

Johanna shook her head, tears falling freely. "I wrote to her. I told her to move on, to live the life she was born to. Her family is wealthy and very traditional—I would never be accepted there. I convinced myself that my only choice was to let her go."

Matron Campbell patted her arm. "Heavens, child, no wonder you're in such a state. I can't say I agree with you making her choice for her, but I understand why you did it."

"What if I made a mistake? What if I lost my best chance at happiness because I'm a bloody fool?"

"Time will tell, but as hard as this is, there's still a war on. You're a strong woman, Johanna, and I don't have to tell you how futile it is to wallow in self-pity. We have a job to do, and I need you at your best. If you need to talk, I'm here, but I expect professionalism when you're on duty."

Johanna straightened her shoulders and wiped her eyes. Matron, with patience and kindness, had given her the chance to unburden herself, and now it was time to buck up and carry on. "I understand, Matron, and…thank you."

❖

July brought waves of wounded from Passchendaele. The men told horror stories of the heavy rains and mud so deep that rifles clogged, tanks floundered, and men and horses drowned. Under constant bombardment, they could do little but hunker down in shell craters full of putrid water, surrounded by mud, rats, and rotting body parts of those that had gone before. Scores of soldiers lost their feet to trench foot so severe, the flesh rotted away to the bone, and nearly every wound was infected. The hospital staff also learned very quickly that chemical warfare had escalated. Soldiers were coming in with massive blisters and burns, blinded and struggling to breathe. The culprit was mustard gas, a horrific new weapon deployed by the Germans.

Word came that more nurses were needed at the casualty clearing stations because too many of the wounded were dying while waiting to be seen. Johanna needed to get away, and she once again volunteered. Hard work was the balm for her shattered heart—the less time she had to think, the better.

"Are you sure you want to do this?" Matron Campbell asked. "You're putting yourself at significant risk. They want reinforcements at Saint-Omer and Brandhoek, right on the rail lines, so you know you'll be directly in the line of fire."

"Aye, I'm aware," Johanna said.

"I could see about transferring you to Calais instead, away from the front."

"No, I'd prefer to go where the greater need is, Matron."

Matron Campbell sighed. "Stubborn as the day is long, you are. I just think you may be doing this for the wrong reasons. I worry that you're being reckless with your life."

Johanna looked her superior in the eye and saw her own worry mirrored there, but she wouldn't be dissuaded. Perhaps Matron was right that she was throwing caution to the wind, but it didn't matter—she'd made up her mind. "With respect, Matron, it's my life and my decision. Send me to Brandhoek."

## CHAPTER TWENTY-ONE

Johanna had stepped into hell on Earth, worse even than Hazebrouck had been. Brandhoek CCS was chaotic, like an anthill that had been violently disturbed. Stretcher bearers, nurses, and orderlies were in constant motion, trying desperately to help the wounded pouring in from Passchendaele. Every single man was caked in foul-smelling muck, and the stench made Johanna retch. As she stood for a moment to get her bearings, a nurse approached and held up a hand in greeting. Her uniform was streaked with mud and blood, but she moved with the tireless energy of someone on a mission.

"Sister, you are one of the reinforcements?"

"Aye, I'm Sister Lennox, just in from Boulogne."

"Glad to meet you. I'm Sister Hawkins. Come, I need to get you up to speed."

Johanna followed the woman to a large tent, outside of which was a decontamination and bathing station. Orderlies were stripping dozens of soldiers of their clothing and ushering them to makeshift showers.

"These men have been exposed to mustard gas," Sister Hawkins explained. "Once they've been washed, they'll come inside. We irrigate their eyes, excise and treat the blisters, then get them into clean clothing. You'll join the rotation with Sisters Jones and Pratt there." She pulled over a medical cart. "Here's the irrigation solution for the eyes—you may need to rinse them several times before there's any relief. We're clipping away all the blistered skin, cleaning the area with this antiseptic lotion, and wrapping with Vaseline gauze."

"What about their lungs?" Johanna said.

"We do whatever we can to get them to cough up the poisoned phlegm—menthol, camphor, eucalyptus. When they do get it up, they are much more comfortable. It's been just awful, Sister. I thought chlorine gas was the worst, until now. This mustard gas burns them even through their clothes, and it doesn't dissipate. You'll need to keep your gas mask handy and mind what you touch."

"Thank you, Sister. Where can I leave my bag?"

"Just there for now. Ready?"

"Ready." Johanna began on one end of the tent, irrigating the burning eyes of one soldier after another. Those that had been farthest away from the exploding gas canisters were able to stand or sit elsewhere after treatment, vacating the beds for the more seriously affected. Johanna was shocked at the size of the blisters, sometimes covering the length of a man's body. They were yellow, pus-filled, and extremely painful. Some of the men's faces had been protected by their respirators, but their bodies bore the brunt of the exposure.

"Thank you, Sister," the men said, one after the other, as she relieved their pain as gently as she could. An overwhelming anger welled up inside her, making her hands shake. She couldn't rid her mind of all the horrific wounds she'd seen. What had the world gained from all this?

Twenty-eight hours later, Johanna fell exhausted onto a cot in the nurses' tent. The guns boomed in the distance, rattling her nerves and making her head ache. The only thing in the world that could calm her was the voice and touch of a woman whom she'd never see again. Futile tears soaked the pillow beneath her head, until there were no more left to cry.

❖

France seemed like a million miles away to Ellie now, because Johanna was there and wasn't answering her letters. Unable to reach her, Ellie was frustrated and fearful. What was going through Johanna's mind? Why would she throw away what they had? What if something had happened to her? Two months had gone by with no word, and not knowing was taking its toll.

"I expected you to have bounced back a bit more by now, Eleanor," Dr. Phipps said. He had been their family physician all of Ellie's life, and he now sat with her in the parlor after the latest checkup. Thankfully, her mother had gone into London with Papa for the day and wasn't eavesdropping.

"I'm fine, Doctor, just tired. I haven't been sleeping well," Ellie said.

"Have your nightmares continued?" She, like so many others, relived the horrors of the war in her dreams.

"Yes, but not as frequently." Lately, her worry for Johanna disrupted her sleep far more often.

"I can give you a sleeping draught if you'd like. Your lungs sound clear, but it may take several more months for you to regain your full strength. Are you going for walks as we discussed?"

"Yes, I walk around the gardens or to the orchard and back, but I still get winded fairly quickly," Ellie responded.

"Unfortunately, that's to be expected."

Ellie sighed. "I guess there's no chance of me rejoining my Voluntary Aid Detachment, then."

"Heavens, no," the doctor said, his bushy white eyebrows shooting straight into his hairline. "Why would you want to go back?"

Ellie thought about the long hours, the mangled bodies, the extreme cold and heat, the lice, the stench, but none of that mattered. "I was useful there, Doctor, and everything I did made a difference," she said. "Every time I have to sit through one of Mother's frivolous little tea parties, I want to scream. You must know what I mean."

The doctor chuckled. "Yes, young lady, I do, though I'm happy to have a good reason to keep you here where it's safe. Your mother is a creature of habit, as are most of her friends, my wife included. But in this difficult time, routine is likely what keeps them from going mad with worry."

Ellie hadn't thought of it that way, and she softened a little. "I also have a dear friend there whom I can't reach, and I'm concerned for her. Should I write to the matron and inquire?"

"Don't see why not," Dr. Phipps said. "Now, I must be going. Mind my instructions, Eleanor. You cannot rush your recovery."

"All right, I'll behave. Thank you, Doctor."

As soon as he left, Ellie began drafting a letter to Matron Campbell. With any luck, she'd hear something back about Johanna. She clung to this slim hope, because she couldn't bear to think of the alternative.

❖

Several days later, as she sat with her parents eating breakfast, the butler brought the mail.

"Here's one for you, Ellie," Papa said.

Ellie's heart skipped a beat as she took the envelope. The handwriting was unfamiliar. Too impatient to wait, she opened the letter with trembling hands.

*Dear Miss Winthrop,*

*I received your letter and am so pleased to hear you are doing well. I cannot help but tell you, though, that your excellent work is sorely missed here. We, of course, will carry on until the end.*

*Please do not be alarmed, but I am aware that Sister Lennox stopped communication with you, and why. She has convinced herself that she was right to do so, but it pains me to think of how you both must feel. You should know that nurses were again called up to the front, and she went. I imagine she will be unhappy that I've told you, but if I were in your shoes, I should want to know. She is at CCS Brandhoek, near Ypres, for the foreseeable future, as they were in dire need of more nurses. I don't know if hearing from you now would be a help or a hindrance to her, hell-bent as she was to leave this place behind. I've no idea when I'll see her again, but if I can, I will be sure to let you know of her welfare.*

*Forgive my boldness, but I advise you to be patient. Sister Lennox is stubborn, but a truer heart never beat. When this war is over, perhaps you will find each other again.*

*With warmest regards,*
*Matron Fiona Campbell*

"Eleanor, what is it?" Mother said.

Ellie wiped her eyes. "It's nothing. Please excuse me." She rose from the table, feeling the weight of her parents' eyes on her, and walked out, her sparks of worry for Johanna now a raging inferno. What had made her confide in Matron Campbell, and what was she running away from now?

## CHAPTER TWENTY-TWO

Johanna?" A mud-covered soldier stepped toward her, nearly unrecognizable but for one thing—the bright blue eyes that smiled down at her.

"Oh my God, Theo!" She moved to embrace him, but he held up a hand.

"Don't. I'm beyond filthy, if you haven't noticed. Just spent the last hour scraping layers of muck off our horses' legs. The poor beasts can barely walk. What are you doing here?"

"They needed help, if you haven't noticed," she said, smiling for the first time in what felt like forever. "I can't tell you how good it is to see you. How's the hand?"

Theo grimaced. "The rest of it's still there, but it's stiff and hurts like the devil sometimes. Nothing like what these fellows have to bear, though." He gestured toward the rows of stretchers on the ground, holding burned and broken men. "We were sent here with two other transport units. Seems modern conveyances can't hold a candle to good old-fashioned horse power in this mud. Even so, we lost three this week alone." He ran his hand through his hair, and Johanna could see it trembling. "Damn shame. These animals give their all to us and will work until they drop."

"Sister, water," someone gasped nearby.

"Theo, I have to go. Will you be here awhile?"

"I've ordered a rest for the horses, at least twenty-four hours if we can get away with it. They'll be no use to us otherwise. Will you have a break at all?"

"Who knows?" Johanna flinched when a whizbang landed on the other side of the rail line, not five hundred meters away. "Depends on how busy the Germans will be tonight. If I can, I'll come find you. You've lifted my spirits, I can tell you."

"Likewise, dear Sister," he replied, bowing formally.

A laugh bubbled up from Johanna's throat, the sound strange to her ears. "You look ridiculous."

He grinned, his teeth a stark white in his dirt-blackened face. "And you look like an angel."

An image of Ellie popped into Johanna's head, causing an ache so powerful she gasped. "You're wrong," she said. "There are no angels here."

After several more hours of tending to the wounded, Johanna was finally relieved for a rest. Despite being bone-tired, she went in search of Theo. He was with the unscathed members of his unit on the western edge of the camp, watching the farrier clean a horse's hooves.

"Theo," she said, and he smiled, looking so much like Ellie she nearly hugged him. He had cleaned up a bit, and his too long red hair stuck up at odd angles, making him look like a schoolboy.

"You should be resting, Sister Lennox, but I won't pretend to be sorry you're here. Come, let's get you off your feet." He threw a gray horse blanket over a bale of hay and motioned for Johanna to sit.

She sank down onto the makeshift seat with a groan. "Thank you. How are the horses?"

"Most are perking up a bit, but two are lame. I'm hoping more rest and some poultices on the knees will cure them. I'll be leaving one of my drivers here to tend them when we head out tomorrow."

"Och, you'll not have much of a rest, then."

"We'll manage," he said. "Can't sit about idle when there are wounded to be brought in."

Johanna noticed once again the slight trembling of Theo's hands and the strain on his face. "How are you holding up out there? The horses aren't the only ones suffering, I reckon."

Theo's shoulders sagged for the briefest of moments. "It's bloody awful out there, if you want the truth. When it gets particularly bad, I console myself with the knowledge that our work is saving lives. I imagine you must do the same, eh?"

Johanna nodded. The scope of pain and death was great and could easily overwhelm the mind. "I've learned to focus on the details in front of me—assess the damage, bandage this, clean that, give an injection, then go to the next one. It's the only way I can keep on."

"Just so, but enough of all that, now. Let's talk about more pleasant topics. Lately I've been thinking about what I'd most like to eat. For me, it's one of Cook's raspberry tarts with clotted cream. How about you?"

The last decent meal Johanna had eaten was the bouillabaisse she and Ellie shared in Paris. Good God, did everything have to come back to memories of her? She shrugged. "I don't know. Anything fresh that hasn't come in a tin, I suppose."

"Right."

Theo was quiet for a bit, and they sat watching the men tend to the horses. Johanna was so tired she nearly drifted off right on that bale of hay.

"Say, have you heard from Ellie lately?" Theo said.

The question startled her, piercing through the fog of fatigue, and she felt the familiar ache. He couldn't know that the merest thought of Ellie brought her pain. She schooled her features as best she could. "I haven't. You?"

"Had a letter from her a month ago. Old Doc Phipps is making her rest, but she's chomping at the bit to be out and about. If I know my sister, she's probably going stir-crazy."

Johanna knew she shouldn't ask more, but her traitorous mouth forged ahead. "What will she be up to, now she's back home?"

"Oh, probably giving Mother fits. You know, keeping company with suffragettes and balking against the tidy box she is expected to fit in. Ellie is stubborn, smart, and knows her mind. Growing up with her has ruined me for all the sweet little girls back home who can't step over a puddle on their own. She really is quite amazing, but if you tell her I said so, I shall never speak to you again."

Johanna marveled at Theo's humor in the midst of these darkest of days. She had grown quite fond of him in their short acquaintance and thought of him as a rare friend. It made letting go of Ellie even harder.

"Tell me about you," Theo said. "Have you got a lucky bloke somewhere?"

"Me? Heavens, no," Johanna said, feeling herself blush. "Nursing has taken all my time these last few years." Not to mention that loving Ellie had cured her of ever wanting a bloke.

"That's a shame," Theo said. He gazed at her, head cocked to the side, as if seeing her for the first time. "You're a fine woman, Sister Lennox."

Johanna blinked at him for a moment. She hadn't seen this coming. "Are you flirting with me, Lieutenant?"

Theo at least had the grace to look embarrassed. "Um, I wouldn't say flirting, exactly." He stared at his boots, and Johanna felt a surge of affection for him. She knew how badly the men needed the comfort and companionship of women. The shocking rate of syphilis among the soldiers meant many of them found it wherever they could.

"Good. I wouldn't want to spoil our friendship." She smiled to soften her words. "I would love to talk some more, but I really need some rest. Find me before you leave?"

Theo nodded. "I will. And," he said, grinning, "thanks for letting me down easy."

Johanna chuckled. "As my granny used to say, *Yer aff yer heid.*"

Theo laughed. "My grandfather always said, *Don't be daft.* Those old folks were harsh."

A shell exploded in the near distance and Johanna flinched. "I'm just glad they're not here to see this."

❖

As the battle at Passchendaele raged on, the casualty clearing station staff worked nonstop to keep up with the wounded. Johanna continued to provide whatever care she could to the men, but inside she was numb. Even in sleep, she never relaxed, and she wondered if she ever would again.

The Germans had been bolder in their attacks near the rail line, where troop transport and ambulance trains came and went frequently. The booming and banging of artillery, the moans and screams of men, the rattle and rumble of wagons and motors became the musical score to this macabre tragedy.

Johanna was on triage, sorting the mostly alive from the mostly dead. Stretching her back for a moment, she looked up at the night sky. It was clear, a million stars shining and a full moon chasing away the shadows. Such a night helped her work, but she felt a sudden sense of foreboding, because such a night was also ideal for aerial bombing. She worked as fast as she could, tagging some for immediate surgery, some for chemical burn treatment, and others to be cleaned up and loaded onto the waiting ambulance train for transport to a base hospital.

"Sister Lennox, I'll take over here," the head nurse called from her left. "I need you on dressings inside."

Johanna nodded and went into the tent, where two other sisters were cutting off mud-brown uniforms to expose mud-brown and blood-red field dressings. They fell into a rhythm—strip off clothing, give the man a quick wash, remove the soiled dressings, clean and disinfect the wound, apply clean dressings, give a saline injection or perhaps morphia, and call for an orderly to move the man to surgery or to the train. Then go to the next, and the next—they just never stopped coming. Every fiber of her being screamed at her to stop, but she couldn't. Nearly every wound was infected, full of pus and maggots—the longer the soldiers waited for treatment, the greater the chance that they would die.

A nearby explosion shook the ground, rattling the tent and extinguishing the lanterns. In the next moment, Johanna's world began moving in slow motion. She felt her eardrums burst and she was lifted off the ground, as if a giant hand had picked her up and thrown her aside like a rag doll. Pain exploded in her shoulder and cheek, and then she was floating. A deep calm settled over her, and everything faded to nothingness.

## CHAPTER TWENTY-THREE

*One month later*

"I can't understand why you insist on being rude to those gentlemen," Mother said over breakfast. "It's embarrassing to keep sending them away with no good explanation."

"Why should you be embarrassed, Mother? They're not looking to marry you," Ellie said.

"Well, I'm the only woman in my circle with a twenty-four-year-old unmarried daughter, that's why. People talk, you know."

Ellie felt her face flush as her temper flared. "So you would have me marry some old codger whom I can barely stand, let alone love, just so your lady friends won't look down on you? My happiness apparently isn't a factor here."

"If you're waiting around for love and happiness to find you, you most assuredly will be an old maid. A woman of your station is expected to marry well and have children—that's all there is to it."

Ellie had heard enough. "I'm sure Papa would love to hear your views on a happy marriage. At any rate, Mother, you can bloody well take your expectations and feed them to the pigs."

"Eleanor Winthrop!"

"The war has taught me, among other things, that life is too short to settle, and I'd rather be alone than stuck in an unhappy marriage just because someone expects it of me." Despite the shock and disapproval on her mother's face, Ellie plowed on. "I hope I've made myself clear, Mother, for I shan't receive even one more gentleman caller. I shall decide with whom I spend my time."

Ellie's heart pounded—she'd stood her ground, and it felt incredible. She watched her mother sputter and fuss, but this time, she wouldn't give in.

"I don't know when you became so contrary and disrespectful. I thought I had raised a daughter who knew her place and her duty."

"Mother, if you think I am any different now than I've ever been, you haven't been paying attention." Ellie walked to the door. "I'm going out. Good-bye."

She grabbed her coat and called for the car. She'd learned to drive during her long convalescence, since walking to the village had become too taxing. Guilt prickled in her belly over how she had spoken to her mother, but the rush of exhilaration, of empowerment, squelched any feelings of unease.

Ellie needed to connect with Johanna, to share this moment. She knew Johanna believed she would fall prey to her mother's expectations and had ended their budding romance out of fear. Ellie blamed herself—she never should have written so carelessly about her mother's matchmaking attempts. Johanna, who had already lost so much, had taken a huge risk with her heart, and Ellie had ruined everything.

Stifling a sob, she climbed into the car and waited for Bailey to crank the engine. Before he did, he came around to peer in the driver's side window.

"Excuse me, miss, but are you feeling poorly?" The look on his kind old face touched her, and she reached out to pat his arm.

"Oh, Bailey, I'm fine, just feeling a bit melancholy."

"It's your time in France that haunts you, I think," he said. "Forgive my boldness, but I've been keeping my eye on you since you've been back. It's plain to see you had a rough go."

"It's the memories—some days are harder than others." It's the closest she had come to speaking of the war in months.

"Oh yes, miss, I reckon I know a thing or two about that," Bailey said, nodding. "Even at my age, I can still remember what it was like to fight a war. I lost many a good mate in South Africa, but it was the camps that took a piece of my soul."

Ellie looked at him in surprise. He'd never spoken much about anything personal, but she could see in his eyes that he needed to share. She felt honored that he had chosen her. "The camps?" she said.

"They made us destroy everything—homes, crops, livestock—and then use their soldiers' families against them. The scorched-earth policy, they called it. We drove Boer women and children into camps. Thousands of innocents died in those camps—it's the starving children more than anything else that I can't forget."

"I'm sorry, Bailey. I guess every war has its horrors," Ellie said, shuddering. "There are so many burdens to carry now."

"I'm an old man, Miss Ellie. Getting too tired to shoulder them anymore." Bailey touched his cap. "I thank you, young lady—I've not spoken of such things to anyone in many years, not even my own wife. You're a fine listener and you've eased my mind."

Ellie nodded, too choked up to speak. Bailey went round to the front of the car and cranked the engine. As she pulled away, she waved to the dear man and focused on the road ahead. She had no destination in mind, but she needed to drive until the ache in her heart subsided.

❖

Johanna lurched upright at the loud bang and cried out as pain lanced through her shoulder. Her heart pounded as she searched for the source of the sound. Across the room, a volunteer was picking up metal trays from the tile floor.

"Sorry, Sister," the VAD said, her face scarlet.

Joanna groaned and lay back on her pillow. The girl was sweet but clumsy as a drunken sailor.

"What time is it?" Her voice was still thick and muffled, as if she had a mouthful of cotton.

"Almost noontime, Sister. They'll be bringing round the meal soon. Can I get you anything until then?"

"Aye, some tea would be nice." Johanna had been transferred here from the hospital in Calais two weeks ago, and she was beyond grateful to be on home soil. Still, the war had followed her, haunting her sleep and filling her waking hours with pain.

There'd been an air raid, they said, on the rail line at Brandhoek. A wayward bomb had landed on one end of the tent Johanna had been in, the blast throwing her across the ward, injuring her and killing a nurse along with several of the men they'd worked so hard to save. She had a dislocated shoulder, shrapnel wounds in her thigh and cheek, and a severe concussion. She was lucky to be alive, they'd said. Johanna wasn't so sure.

A heavy dark mood had overtaken her since she'd been in hospital. Working had made her feel alive, had kept her grief at bay. Without it, she didn't know who she was. She lifted her hand to touch the bandage on her face. They hadn't told her how bad the wound was, but she would surely have a nasty scar. After the war, would anyone want to hire a disfigured woman? Would she be left to beg on the streets of Edinburgh?

"I need to get out of here," Johanna said, feeling like she was crawling out of her own skin.

"But Sister," the volunteer said, "the doctor said you mustn't be up and about just yet."

"I don't much care what the doctor said. I'll lose my bloody mind just lying here, so you can help me or deal with the consequences."

The girl gaped at her for a moment, then rushed out of the room. She returned moments later with a wheelchair.

"That's a good lass. Now, help me get into it." After some painful maneuvering, she was upright and sitting in the chair. "Take me where there's a view of something other than white walls."

"One moment, Sister." The volunteer stepped away and spoke to the charge nurse, who looked at Johanna and nodded.

The volunteer, Molly, wheeled Johanna along a corridor and onto a lift, which took them down to the ground floor. The building was formerly a primary school, and a few of its offices and classrooms had been converted into sitting rooms. One small section had been designated for the handful of female patients, who were to be kept separate from the men. As Molly wheeled her swiftly past a room full of convalescents, they heard a loud voice.

"Ho, there, is that a sister?"

Molly gasped and sped up, but Johanna stopped her. "It's all right, Molly. Let me talk to the men."

"But I'm not supposed to…"

"Stay with me, then, if you think I need a chaperone. I want to talk to the men."

Molly threw up her hands but complied, wheeling Johanna into the room.

"Ah, Sister, Fritz got you, too?" Nine eager faces turned to her, and she smiled as best she could.

"Aye, but he missed a few parts."

The men roared with laughter, and Johanna felt her spirits rise. She understood these men, and they her. Only someone who'd been over there could fully comprehend what they'd experienced together.

"Where were you, Sister?"

"Boulogne at first, at a general hospital. But this happened at CCS Brandhoek, near Passchendaele," she said, indicating her bandages.

"I was there. My leg's probably stuck in the mud somewhere, but I got me a shiny new one," a young man said, tapping his prosthetic with a cane.

The men took turns sharing stories, and Johanna told her own. As the time passed, her heavy mantle of despair grew lighter. These wounded soldiers treated her like one of their own and focused on her humanity, not her broken bits. Maybe there would be a place for her in this world after all.

❖

Ellie took breakfast in her room the next day. Her mother was still in a snit, and Ellie hadn't the patience for it. Yesterday's show of independence might have upset Mother, but Ellie felt renewed with an energy, a purpose, that she hadn't had in months.

A knock sounded at the door. "Who is it?" Ellie called, in case it was her mother coming to fuss at her again.

"It's Jones, miss."

"Oh, come in." Ellie smiled when the young maid entered. "How are you today?"

Jones, as usual, looked surprised to be asked. "I'm just fine, miss, thank you. Mail's come for you." She produced a letter and handed it to Ellie.

"Thank you," Ellie said, her heart skipping when she saw the return address.

"Will you be needing anything else, miss?"

"If you like, you can take the breakfast tray. I've finished."

"Very good, miss." Jones took the tray and left the room.

Ellie had written to Matron Campbell every month, hoping for word on Johanna. Now she opened the envelope, praying that this was the news she'd been waiting for.

*Dear Miss Winthrop,*

*I hope this letter finds you in good health. I've received a report on Sister Lennox, which is both distressing and hopeful. There was an attack on her location some weeks ago, and she was wounded. I hesitated to tell you until I knew of her condition. I can now report that she is back in Scotland, recovering at a hospital in Edinburgh. I don't know the name of the facility, but I trust your investigative skills will uncover the information you seek.*

*I wish you the best of luck, and would welcome any bit of good news if you choose to share it. God willing, all of us here will be on our way home soon. Until then, take care of yourself.*

*Yours truly,*
*Matron Fiona Campbell*

"Oh my God, she's only a few hours from here. I've got to go to her."

Ellie jumped up, then sat again as a sobering thought came. She'd have to have a good explanation to get around her parents and Dr. Phipps. What she needed was a plan.

## CHAPTER TWENTY-FOUR

I think I'll be taking a little trip for a few days," Ellie said at dinner the next evening.

"Oh? What for?" her father said.

"A dear friend of mine is back from the war. She's had a terrible time of it, and I'd like to look in on her."

"Well, surely a visit won't require a few days," her mother put in.

"She's in Edinburgh, Mother." Ellie tried to remain calm, but her stomach was in knots.

"Why on earth would you want to travel to Scotland at this time of year? It'll be cold and damp, and in your condition—"

"My condition is much improved. I'm perfectly capable of sitting while the train does all the hard work."

"Now, Ellie, your mother is only concerned about your health," her father said, but the twinkle in his eye belied his chastising tone. "Who is this friend?"

"She's a nurse, Papa. We were in the same hospital in Boulogne, and she helped train me," Ellie replied.

"Does this nurse have a name? I know some families in Edinburgh."

*Bloody hell.* "It's Johanna, Johanna Lennox."

"Hmm. Doesn't ring a bell. What does her father do?"

"Her parents have both passed on. That's why I'd like to go. She may be in need of some assistance," Ellie said, daring now to hope.

"I suppose it would be all right," her father said.

"But Charles, is it wise for young ladies to travel alone? It seems so dangerous these days," Mother said.

"Ellie's been in far more dangerous places than Edinburgh, my dear, and she's not a child anymore." Mother pressed her lips together but said nothing further—she wouldn't contradict her husband.

"Thank you, Papa. Shall I go into London with you to purchase the ticket?" Ellie said, tamping down her excitement.

"If you can be ready. I'll be leaving shortly," he replied.

"Yes, just give me ten minutes."

Ellie rushed off to her room, shut the door, and grabbed her pillow, into which she proceeded to scream with joy.

"Oh, Johanna, my darling, I'll be with you soon."

As the train rumbled north, Ellie went over the plan in her head. She would need to find a room upon arriving, then begin the search for hospitals. Perhaps the local Red Cross would be a good place to start. Then once she found Johanna...Ellie's stomach lurched as a new thought crept in. Johanna had told her to move on, but what if Johanna herself had found someone new?

She shook her head, unwilling to despair over something that might never come to pass. She would find Johanna, convince her of her devotion, and hope for the best. Ellie had no information about the extent of Johanna's injuries—was she infirm, shell-shocked, an amputee? The unknown consumed her thoughts for the rest of the journey, and before she knew it, she had arrived at Princes Street Station.

Late autumn in Edinburgh was as cold and damp as her mother had predicted. Ellie turned up her coat collar against the icy wind and made her way to The Caledonian Hotel, but thought better of it. She needed to be careful of her money, for she did not want to ask her father for more. She walked on and found a much more affordable hotel, where she booked a room. A bit winded from her walk in the cold, Ellie took a rest before heading back down to the concierge.

"Excuse me, sir. I've come to Edinburgh to find a woman friend who is in hospital. I don't know which one—can you tell me where I might start looking?"

"Aye, miss. If your friend is a woman, you'd best start at Bruntsfield, though it will be a fair walk. Shall I call for a taxicab?" he said.

"Yes, please."

Ellie was relieved not to have to walk about the city. A motor taxi arrived and she was on her way, anxious to begin her search for Johanna. Trying to tamp down her emotions, she focused on the passing city. Edinburgh Castle rose up above the streets, majestic and untouched, unlike so many other ancient landmarks in war-torn Europe. People bustled about, tending to their daily business, as if the world wasn't being blown to smithereens just a day's travel away.

"Miss, here is Bruntsfield," the driver said.

"Thank you," Ellie said, paying him. She stepped out in front of a large four-story stone building with tall dormers along the top floor. Ellie stepped through the iron gate and entered the hospital, her heart racing.

Inside, there was the steady hum of a busy hospital—low voices in conversation, the clatter of cart wheels on the tile floor, a baby crying. Ellie walked along a wide corridor until she found the main nurses' station. A gray-haired nurse standing behind the long counter looked up and smiled.

"Good afternoon. How may I help you?"

"Good afternoon. I'm trying to locate a friend who was wounded in France and is in hospital somewhere in Edinburgh. I was told to inquire here," Ellie said.

The nurse frowned. "Oh, I'm sorry, ma'am, but this is the women's and children's hospital. We have no war wounded here."

"But my friend is a woman, a nurse. She was wounded in the line of duty. Where else would she be?"

"Wounded? My goodness. Well, she won't be at City Hospital—they take the infectious disease patients over there. I've heard tell of several auxiliary hospitals and convalescent homes springing up all over Britain, to handle the wounded soldiers coming home, but I don't reckon they take female patients. Was your friend with the Scottish Women's Hospitals overseas?"

"No, the Red Cross," Ellie said, swallowing the panic that had begun to rise. *What if I can't find her?*

"They ought to have a record of her at headquarters, then. Their building is near the city center, just past St. Giles' Cathedral. You know the place?"

Ellie shook her head, feeling very much the outsider. "I'm afraid I don't, though I thank you for the information. Could you ring for a taxi, if it isn't too much trouble?"

"Aye, ma'am, and good luck finding your friend, the poor lass."

By the time the taxi came and took Ellie across town, the Red Cross headquarters had closed for the day. She wanted to scream in frustration, but a fat lot of good that would do. With a plan to resume her search first thing in the morning, Ellie went back to her hotel room, where the long night of waiting loomed before her. The thought that, for all she knew, Johanna could be as close as the next street over drove her to distraction. *Oh, for God's sake, you haven't seen her in months. What's one more night?* She scolded herself to be patient, but the minutes ticked by with agonizing slowness, and sleep wouldn't come.

As Johanna recovered, she worried more and more about what the future would bring. She had no home—after her mother's death, she had sold their tiny flat and had a little money set aside, but not much. She was unsure of her employment status as well, especially now. When the war ended, thousands of nurses would be returning home, and many would still work in the field. Would she be able to find a job? The uncertainty stole her sleep and her appetite, dominating her thoughts more than anything except...

Ellie. That blue-eyed angel had turned her world upside down, and she would never be the same. Their relationship had awakened Johanna to her true nature, something she had never known or considered before. The love of a woman was what she needed, but Ellie was who she wanted. Johanna's heart ached with missing her, and now that she had time to think, she wondered if she'd been too hasty in pushing Ellie away. Thanks to her stubborn foolishness, Ellie was probably married now, and they'd never meet again. That pain hurt deeper than any of her wounds.

"Sister Lennox?"

Johanna, caught daydreaming, turned in her chair with a start. "Aye?"

The volunteer smiled. "You have a visitor."

"A visitor? Who...?" She glanced past the woman and time stopped. In the doorway, wearing a blue cashmere coat and an uncertain smile, was Ellie.

"Oh my God." Johanna felt like she used to when her father's boat would crest a large swell—exhilarated and terrified at the same time. She rose from the chair, never taking her eyes off the vision before her.

"Hello, Johanna," Ellie said, stepping closer. "It's so very good to see you."

They stared at each other for several beats in awkward silence until the volunteer took the hint and left. Ellie closed the gap in two quick strides and took Johanna's hands in hers, tears streaming down her cheeks.

"I can't believe you're here," Johanna said, her own tears flowing. "How did you know?"

"Matron Campbell. She sent word as soon as she learned what had happened to you." Ellie brushed her thumb near the bandage on Johanna's cheek. "Oh, Johanna, are you all right?"

"I'll heal. And how are you?"

"Much better now I'm here. I missed you so awfully," Ellie said, her voice breaking.

"You came all this way to find me, even after what I wrote to you?"

"You can't get rid of me that easily, Johanna Lennox." Ellie embraced her and whispered, "Don't you know I love you?"

The dam burst, and Johanna wept in Ellie's arms. "I'm so sorry." She pulled back, wincing. "I have to sit."

"Tell me what happened," Ellie said, as Johanna eased back into her chair.

"A bomb fell on the hut I was working in. I was thrown by the blast, and my left side took the brunt of it," Johanna said. "I don't remember much—I took a hard knock to the head."

"Thank God it wasn't worse. Why did you go so close to the front?" Ellie said.

Johanna looked away. "I was off my head. I convinced myself that I had to give you up, and without you, my life didn't seem so important anymore."

Ellie cupped Johanna's cheek, wiping her tears away. "I was very angry with you, you know."

Johanna nodded. "Matron Campbell told me I was wrong to make your decision for you."

"That's right. All my life people have told me what to do, where to go, who to be. I couldn't bear that from you, too."

"I'm so sorry, Ellie."

Ellie sighed. "How did Matron Campbell become a part of all this?"

Johanna smiled at the memory. "She said she knew I was moping around and miserable because you'd left, and that I needed to snap out of it and do my job. But she also told me that before the war, she had a relationship like ours. She understood me, Ellie. Her support meant everything."

Ellie's heart filled with gratitude. "In her letter, she said she hoped we'd find one another again. I must write and tell her you're all right."

Johanna gazed into Ellie's eyes. "I feel like this is a dream. Thoughts of you gave me comfort in my worst moments, but to touch you again is heaven."

"My darling, I'm here now. This is real."

Voices in the corridor grew louder as they approached the room. Moments later, a white-coated doctor entered the room.

"Sister Lennox, how are you feeling today?"

"Much better, Doctor."

"The headaches?"

"Mostly gone."

"Splendid, splendid. That shoulder needs to remain immobile for a while longer, but I do believe it's time to send you home," the doctor said.

Johanna blanched. "I've no home to go to just yet."

"Oh, dear. You have no family to take over your care?"

"No, Doctor, but I'll manage."

"Excuse me, Doctor. I'm Eleanor Winthrop, a friend, and I've taken a room on Princes Street indefinitely. With her permission, I would be happy to provide care and lodging for Sister Lennox until she is back on her feet."

"But, Ellie, that's far too much to ask," Johanna protested, eyes wide.

"You're not asking, I'm offering, and it would be my pleasure," Ellie said.

"You understand that she still needs assistance with wound care and some daily activities. Could you help with that?"

"Oh yes, Doctor. I served in a general hospital in France and was trained by the best," Ellie said, giving Johanna a wink.

"Well, that sounds like a fine idea to me, then," the doctor said, clapping his hands together. "Shall I draw up the discharge papers?"

Johanna looked at Ellie, unable to believe this sudden turn of events. Ellie nodded with a smile, and it was settled. "Yes, please, Doctor. I'm ready."

## CHAPTER TWENTY-FIVE

Ellie supported Johanna with one arm and carried her belongings in the other as they entered the hotel. The concierge rushed to assist, and soon Johanna had settled in. The room had two beds, a sitting area, and its own separate lavatory. Johanna sat propped up on one of the beds, her wounded leg resting on a pillow.

"I still can't believe you're doing all this," she said, looking about the room. "It must be quite expensive to stay here."

"You needn't worry about all that," Ellie said. "I brought enough to cover the room for a month—hopefully by then we'll have other accommodations."

"A month? My God, Ellie, your kindness is overwhelming." Johanna suddenly realized what she had heard. "Did you say *we'll* have other accommodations?"

Ellie smiled. "We have a great deal to discuss, Sister Lennox," she said, "but my first priority is making sure you heal up good as new."

Johanna looked away as prickles of anxiety poked at her brain. "Och, Ellie, I'll never be good as new. I'm damaged, scarred. Every day I fear the pain inside will never go away."

Ellie took her hand. "You aren't alone, Johanna. Countless people will bear the scars of this damnable war, but we can get through it together."

"Why would you want to be here playing nursemaid when you could be living your life back home?" Johanna said. She looked at Ellie in time to see her eyes flash with anger.

"Listen, you mule-headed woman. I am not playing nursemaid—I'm choosing to care for the woman I love, and this, right here, is what I want living my life to look like. I lost you once, and I will not let you push me away again."

Johanna flushed hot under Ellie's chastisement, her eyes stinging with tears. "Oh, Ellie, I can't provide you the life you deserve to live, and what about your family? Would they not disown you for being with me?"

Ellie went to Johanna and took her face in her hands. "Look at me. I will ask you this only once, and I want the truth."

Johanna nodded, silenced by the fierce determination in Ellie's eyes.

"Do you love me and want me in your life?"

Her tears finally spilled onto Ellie's hands. "Desperately."

Ellie held her face firmly and looked her directly in the eye. "Then nothing and no one will keep us apart. My family, and anyone else who believes they have a say in the matter, are sadly mistaken if they think otherwise."

"You are bold and brave, two of the many things I adore about you, but family is everything, Ellie, especially now. I lost mine—I cannot ask you to risk losing yours, too."

"If they love me, they won't make me choose."

"Oh, Ellie, is it ever as easy as that? That's why I'm so afraid."

"Afraid of what, love?"

"Your family, the world you come from, will put great pressure on you. I was miserable without you, but I thought it was best to make a clean break so you wouldn't have to choose. Now, I could be selfish and beg you to stay, but I'm afraid that you would come to resent me. I couldn't bear that."

Ellie sighed and moved away. She paced the room in silence, and Johanna's heart broke as she steeled herself for Ellie's response.

"You're right, Johanna. This is a big decision, perhaps the biggest of my life, but I'm asking you to trust that I know my own mind. I am committed to staying here until you are back on your feet, and I want us to get to know each other, away from the craziness of war. If, after a month's time, we feel differently, I'll leave. Can you agree to that?"

Ellie stood, hands on hips, looking strong and so beautiful, and Johanna fell in love all over again. "Aye, Miss Winthrop. I agree."

Ellie smiled and went to her. "Let's seal it with a kiss, shall we?" Their tender kiss soon deepened, full of all the passion they'd held inside for so long. Johanna moaned and shifted, and Ellie pulled back, breathless. "Oh, my darling, have I hurt you?" she said, as if reminded now of Johanna's injuries.

Johanna looked down at her immobilized arm and grinned. "I'm a wee bit sore, but I'll gladly endure it for another kiss."

Ellie laughed. "Pace yourself, love. Perhaps we'd better focus on finding some supper."

"If you insist."

❖

The next two weeks were spent finding a rhythm in their new cohabitation. Johanna's previously dislocated shoulder was still painful, and she needed assistance to dress. The bandage on her thigh wound required changing twice a day, and she suffered headaches after too much noise or activity. Ellie had been a godsend, helping Johanna regain her mobility and independence while providing the care she needed. Even better, they'd spent hours talking about their lives before the war and reliving their experiences in France. They'd kissed and touched, but had yet to make love again.

"You have a wonderful touch, Miss Winthrop," Johanna said as Ellie was tending to her leg. "Much better than my nurse at the hospital. She poked and prodded at me too much."

"Thank you, Miss Lennox. I'm not fond of poking and prodding," Ellie replied, running her hand down Johanna's leg. "I far prefer stroking and caressing." She trailed her fingers down to her ankle and up the other side of her leg, stopping just short of her groin.

Johanna sucked in a breath. "Is this how you treat all your patients?"

"Oh no. Just the beautiful Scottish ones." Ellie grinned and planted a playful kiss on Johanna's nose. "Now let me finish bandaging this leg."

"How's it healing?" Johanna asked, craning her neck to try to see the back of her thigh.

"Quite well," Ellie replied. "It has stopped weeping and is no longer swollen around the sutures. The surgeon did a fine job. I think the scarring will be minimal."

"At least I can hide that one," Johanna said, touching her cheek. She still felt self-conscious about the finger-length scar there, despite Ellie's insistence that it wasn't that noticeable.

"I think this makes you even more attractive," Ellie said, touching her face with gentle fingers. "It tells the story of your service and bravery."

"Is that what people will think when they look at me?"

"It's what I think. You're stunning, and I love you."

Johanna attempted a smile. "Thank you, love. I'm just worried that my appearance will hinder my chances to find work."

"I don't see why that should matter. You have impeccable references, and people are much more used to seeing the ravages of war on a body these days." Ellie took Johanna's hand. "We haven't really talked about future employment. Is nursing still what you want to do?"

"Aye, I'd like to continue nursing. It's all I know, other than scaling and gutting fish. The work is satisfying and respectable, and I think I'm good at it. "

"You're better than good—you have a gift," Ellie replied.

"You're biased."

"Maybe a little, but I've watched you work. Any hospital would be lucky to have you. Now, listen, I've been thinking about something, and I'd like your opinion," Ellie said.

"What is it?"

"I want to complete my own training to become a nurse."

Johanna looked at her in surprise. "You do?"

"Yes. I doubt anything else could be as personally fulfilling, sore feet and aching back aside. But there's more."

Johanna smiled at the look of determination on Ellie's lovely face. "Go on."

"I expect Theo will inherit the family estate, since I won't be marrying, but I happen to know that my father has set aside a sizable sum for me. I want to ask him for the money now—I have a project in mind."

"What kind of project?" Johanna was beginning to feel excited as she watched Ellie's face light up.

"I want to purchase a building and convert it into a long-term convalescent home for returning soldiers, perhaps a special place for those who have severe disfigurement. Some may not have family to care for them, and I want them to live where they are accepted and honored for their sacrifice."

Johanna's eyes widened. "My God, Ellie, you've a heart as big as Britain. What an incredible idea."

"Do you really think so?" Ellie said, her enthusiasm dimming. "I have a tendency to bite off more than I can chew sometimes. I can hear my mother now—she is always saying, *Oh, Eleanor, you and your grand ideas.*"

"I love your grand idea, and I'd love to help," Johanna said, squeezing Ellie's hand.

"I was hoping you'd say that," Ellie said, eyes bright. "If I can manage to turn this idea into reality, I'd like to appoint you Chief Matron. I can think of no one better."

"Just when I think I couldn't possibly love you more, you go and give me a reason," Johanna said, her heart full to bursting.

"Does that mean you'd do it?"

Johanna nodded. "Aye, lass. Count me in."

## CHAPTER TWENTY-SIX

Ellie frowned at the envelope in her hand. She'd sent a quick note to her parents when she'd arrived in Edinburgh so they could reach her if needed, but she hadn't let on that she'd be gone this long. Fully anticipating some backlash, she knew a letter from her mother would arrive eventually. Now that it was in her hands, she hesitated to open it—only her mother could ruin the incredible happiness she'd felt these last weeks.

"Just get it over with," Johanna said, as she stretched and exercised her shoulder. "It could be news of Theo."

Ellie sighed. *Stop being such a baby and open the bloody thing.* Sliding her finger underneath the flap, she drew out her mother's signature ivory stationery and began to read.

*Dear Eleanor,*

*I trust you are well and have completed your business in Edinburgh. Although you evidently decided to extend your holiday, I must ask you to return home. You are a lady of the house, and as such, you are needed here. I've enclosed a return train ticket for Monday morning, which will bring you home in time to help host our annual Ladies' Luncheon. A letter came from Theo this week, which I'm sure you'll be anxious to read. Your father sends his regards. Travel safely.*

*Mother*

Ellie tossed the letter on the bed, her anger rising. "Ugh, that woman!"

"What did she say?" Johanna asked.

Ellie nodded toward the offending object. "See for yourself."

As Johanna read the letter, Ellie paced the room.

"She usually gets her way, I'm guessing," Johanna said.

"Demands it, more like," Ellie said. "She doesn't need help with that luncheon or anything else—the household staff always has everything under control. She just wants me back under her thumb, as if I were still fifteen. And to dangle news of Theo like a damned carrot—oh, she's intolerable."

"What will you do, then?" Johanna said. "She'll be good and mad if you don't use that ticket."

"I honestly don't care. I'm sick to death of her trying to dictate my life." Ellie was livid, and worried. She didn't know how to assert her independence without disrespecting her parents, and her mother could be quite formidable when provoked.

"Ellie, you planned to have a conversation with your father anyway. Maybe you should go back and settle things there. Your mam might be more understanding if you explain your plan for the home—it's a wonderful idea."

"You don't know my mother." Ellie was beside herself. She wanted to be strong, but she was worried that if she went home now, she'd never be able to leave again. Wasn't this exactly what

Johanna had been afraid of? As she mulled over her dilemma, she realized what she had to do.

"I've got to get Papa on my side."

❖

On Monday afternoon, Ellie walked into the bank and took the lift to her father's office. Charles Winthrop sat at his massive oak desk, its surface strewn with ledgers and papers. He was engrossed in writing something, and Ellie took a moment to study him. His thinning hair was grayer than she remembered, his shoulders a bit more stooped. A surge of affection washed over her—she'd missed him.

"Papa."

His startled face broke into a grin. "Ellie, my dear, did you just get in?"

"Yes, not long ago. It's good to see you."

He came from behind his desk and kissed her cheek. "Ah, good to see you as well. How was your holiday in Edinburgh?"

"Wonderful. I have so much to tell you, Papa," Ellie said.

"Have you eaten?"

He shook his head. "I've forgotten, as usual. What say we go to the club for a bite?"

"That would be lovely."

Not long after, they were seated at a table in her father's favorite establishment, enjoying a late lunch. Ellie was nervous—she needed to make her case to Papa before they went back to the house, before her mother got wind of her intentions, but she had no bloody idea where to begin.

"Tell me, Ellie," Papa said, dabbing at his mustache with a napkin. "What kept you away so long? Your mother was driving me mad with her theories of what you'd gotten up to in Scotland."

Papa was smiling, and Ellie took a deep breath. Might as well dive right in. "Well, Papa, it wasn't exactly a holiday. I was helping someone."

"Ah, yes, you mentioned that. A nurse, I believe you said?"

"Yes. Her name is Johanna, and she is a very dear friend. She was wounded in France and needed my help as she recovered."

"That was kind of you, my dear. She's well, then?"

"Mostly. Her family are all dead, and she had nowhere to go. She's been staying with me at the hotel, and we've been looking for a nice flat that she can rent. This really was an inconvenient time for Mother to summon me back."

"Well, you know how she is about her little get-togethers," he said, waving a hand. "Of course, you know she expects you to stay home where you belong."

Ellie's anxiety kicked up a notch at his words, and she had to force herself to breathe. "That's just it, Papa. I don't feel as if I belong there anymore."

"Whatever do you mean?"

"Don't you remember what it was like when you came back from war? How everything you'd known before was different somehow?" Ellie asked.

Her father sighed. "Yes, it was a challenge at first, but everything got back to normal."

"Papa, there is nothing normal about this war. I have seen and done things that have forever changed me. I couldn't possibly go back to the way things were."

"Now, Ellie, in time you'll—"

"No, Papa." Ellie's face burned but her voice remained strong. "I can't fritter away my life at pointless luncheons, talking about the latest fashions. And I can't bear Mother's endless attempts to see me married."

"Your mother just wants what's best for you, Ellie, to be sure you're taken care of."

"Forcing me into a loveless marriage is what's best for me? I'd rather be alone than do that. Now that I've found a purpose, a way to help people, I can't go back to an idle life of leisure. Please understand, Papa—I'm grateful for my life and all you have provided, truly. But now I have a plan, a dream to be of service to others."

Ellie's father looked at her with an odd expression, but in his eyes she detected a hint of pride. "You've always wanted to do things your own way, Ellie. You have your mother's stubbornness, to be sure, but while she struggles with change, you embrace it. I understand that a vibrant young woman such as yourself would not be happy in a marriage of duty or convenience."

"Thank you, Papa."

"Your mother leads a sheltered life, and clinging to the old ways is, for her, a source of comfort and safety. I, however, see every day how this war has upset the natural order of things. London is a different place than it was before, and even if we resist, we'll all eventually be swept along with the tides of change."

Ellie nodded, speechless, a cautious optimism taking root.

Her father continued, "Every day I pray for your brother to return safely, and I think about the future for him and the estate once I'm gone. Perhaps he, too, will want to take a different path." He cleared his throat, his eyes misty. "Life is short, Ellie. What I want for you both, more than anything else, is happiness."

Ellie fought back tears as she reached to take her father's hand. His words had touched and validated her, and she was beyond grateful.

"Now let's get you home," Papa said. "On the way, you can tell me all about this dream of yours."

❖

Armed with her father's blessing, Ellie came to the breakfast table the next morning, ready to talk matters over with her mother. She picked at her food, certain that her nervous stomach would revolt if she ate anything. Her father sat at the head of the table, reading the newspaper, and his presence helped calm Ellie's nerves.

"For heaven's sake, Eleanor, why aren't you eating? Are you ill?" Mother said.

"No, Mother, I'm quite all right. I would like to discuss something with you, though, if you don't mind."

Her mother nodded. "Go on."

"I know you wanted me home to assist with the luncheon today, and I'll happily help with whatever you need. But," Ellie said, pausing to gather her courage, "I won't be staying."

Mother gazed at Ellie over her teacup for a long moment, one eyebrow raised, then slowly returned the cup to its saucer. "What do you mean you won't be staying?"

"I've decided to stay in Edinburgh. I would like to establish a long-term residence for soldiers who have been disabled by the war and have no home or family to care for them."

"Oh, Eleanor, you and your grand ideas," Mother said, and Ellie bit her tongue to check her temper. "I'm sure there are facilities in existence that can help those people. You needn't worry about such things."

"I'm afraid the need is far greater than you realize, Mother. I have found a purpose, and I am passionate about this work. I would like to continue my training to become a nurse, or perhaps even a doctor."

"Oh, posh, a woman doctor! Who has put such nonsense into your head? You'd be wise to forget this foolishness and settle down, Eleanor. There are plenty of nice, eligible men with whom you could be spending your time."

Ellie's face heated as she watched her mother flick a hand in dismissal. "Mother, perhaps you didn't hear me. I am going to Edinburgh to follow my passion, and settling down with a man is not part of the plan."

Her mother put a hand to her chest. "My God, you're serious. Charles, are you listening to this?"

Papa lowered the newspaper and looked his wife in the eye. "Yes, Violet, every word. We have been blessed with a bright, compassionate young woman for a daughter, and I for one fully support her decision."

Mother's mouth dropped open in shock, then just as quickly settled into its habitual frown of disapproval. "I see that I've been left in the dark on this, and my opinion doesn't matter to either of you. If you'll excuse me, I have a luncheon to prepare for. At least I won't be shirking my responsibilities as a lady of this house."

She gathered up her skirt and flounced out of the room.

Ellie's breath came out in a whoosh, and her father grinned. "Wait until she finds out I'm going to Edinburgh to help choose your new building."

Ellie giggled, then sobered. "Oh, Papa, am I making a mistake?"

"My darling daughter, you will never know what you can accomplish until you try."

Ellie jumped up and gave her father a hug. "I love you, Papa. Thank you for your support, especially with Mother. I imagine she'll be upset for a while."

"I've weathered her storms for years. She'll come around eventually." He winked at Ellie. "I hope."

## CHAPTER TWENTY-SEVEN

Johanna couldn't stop smiling as she walked away, the lease to her new flat in hand. It would be available in just a week, and she was excited to move in. She had finally regained some sense of independence, and it felt amazing. They had seen the partially furnished place right before Ellie went back to England, but today, Johanna had signed the papers herself. Ellie had spent a small fortune on the hotel room as Johanna healed. Now that she was mostly recovered, pride dictated that she pay her own way.

Johanna had been busy in the three days Ellie'd been gone. She had made inquiries through the Red Cross and Queen Alexandra's Royal Nursing Service about open posts, and her application had been gratefully accepted. A nurse of her skill was needed, she'd been told, as so many regular nurses had joined the war effort. No one had seemed bothered by her facial scar and slight limp, and Johanna felt encouraged that she'd soon find employment. She couldn't wait to tell Ellie.

As she headed back to the hotel, she suffered another bout of anxiety. What if Ellie ran into trouble with her parents? What if she didn't come back? Johanna tried to push her fears aside— at least she would be able to take care of herself if the worst happened.

It was nearly dinnertime, and Johanna was thinking about where she would eat as she opened the door. She froze in her tracks at the sight before her. Reclining on the bed, in a pale blue satin nightgown, was her beautiful Ellie. Her red-gold hair was loose upon her shoulders, and her lovely smiling face was flushed pink.

"Hello, my darling. I've missed you," Ellie said, standing. The thin material seemed to caress her body as it cascaded down her legs, and Johanna gasped as desire washed over her.

"You came back."

"Of course I came back, love," Ellie replied. "Living without you isn't an option."

"Oh, Christ, Ellie, I was so worried," Johanna said, gathering Ellie's warm body in her arms.

"Everything is fine now, Johanna. I'm here to stay." Ellie reached up and removed the pins from Johanna's hair, running her hands through the tumbling locks. Cupping the back of her head, Ellie placed a tender kiss on Johanna's waiting lips, then blazed a whisper-soft trail along her jaw to her throat, sucking lightly. She dipped her head to capture Ellie's lips again, deepening the kiss with her tongue until they were both breathless and quivering with need. She ran her hands down Ellie's back to her hips, gathering handfuls of satin as she moved back up.

"I need to feel you," she said and drew the nightgown over Ellie's head.

Ellie stood nude, her pale skin blushing under Johanna's worshipful gaze. With trembling fingers, Ellie began to loosen the fastenings of Johanna's dress. Johanna hastened to help, and soon she was naked, her body on fire.

"My love," she said, claiming Ellie's mouth in a searing kiss.

Everywhere Johanna touched was silk, and her hands roamed Ellie's body, coming to rest on her breasts. Ellie's nipples hardened beneath her palms, and her caresses made Ellie whimper with desire.

"You're so beautiful." Johanna took Ellie's hand and led her to the bed. Ellie kissed her, then smiled and lay back, drawing Johanna on top of her.

Their bodies fit perfectly, and Johanna's senses were overwhelmed with pleasure. She buried her face in Ellie's sweet-smelling hair and moved against her. Raising her thigh to meet Johanna's center, Ellie moaned when she reached the warm, wet evidence of Johanna's desire.

"I don't think I can hold back," Johanna said, thrusting her hips.

"Then don't, love. Let go for me."

Johanna leaned forward and braced her arms on either side of Ellie's head, allowing Ellie to suck a taut nipple into her mouth.

"Oh, so good," Johanna cried, thrusting faster. Ellie's thigh was slick and hot, her hands on Johanna's hips urging her closer and closer to the brink.

"Look at me, Johanna," Ellie said.

Johanna gazed down into Ellie's blue eyes, darker now and full of emotion. Ellie brought her hands between them and cupped Johanna's breasts.

"I love you," Ellie said, and she pressed Johanna's breasts together, sucking hard on her swollen nipples. Heat exploded in Johanna's core and radiated throughout her body, leaving her breathless and trembling. She collapsed on top of Ellie, who held her close, stroking her hair and murmuring words of love.

"My God, Ellie, you make me feel so much," Johanna said. "How can I ever express how much I love you?"

"Shh, my love," Ellie said, pressing a finger to Johanna's lips. "I need you to show me."

Johanna kissed Ellie's finger and sucked it gently into her mouth. Ellie moaned and bit her lip, and Johanna's body started to respond all over again. Rolling to Ellie's side, she abandoned the finger and moved to nuzzle her earlobe, leaving tiny kisses in her wake. She cupped one of Ellie's breasts as her mouth found the other, and she licked, sucked, and teased Ellie's nipples until Ellie cried out in pleasure, her hips moving in circles on the bed.

"Touch me, Johanna...oh God, please."

Johanna slid a hand down Ellie's body, stroking and caressing her belly and hips in agonizing avoidance of where Ellie needed her most. She smiled when Ellie whimpered in protest and spread her thighs wide in invitation. Ellie lay open and trusting, her breath coming in shallow pants, her eyes shut and fingers holding Johanna's head to her breast, and Johanna thought this must be what heaven felt like. She touched Ellie then, dipping into her wetness and stroking her folds.

"You're stunning, lass," she said, overcome with her lover's vulnerable beauty. "So ready for me."

"I need...oh!" Ellie's hips came off the bed as Johanna circled her most sensitive spot. Stroking it with her thumb, she slid a finger inside, stunned by Ellie's heat. Another finger joined the first and set up a steady rhythm, drawing Ellie closer to climax. Soon her thighs began to quiver and her belly clenched, her fingers tightening in Johanna's hair.

"I'm so close...don't stop."

Johanna pressed her thumb down firmly and plunged her fingers deep, flicking her nipple with her tongue. Ellie nearly shouted as the orgasm crashed over her, and she rode it for several moments before collapsing, spent.

Johanna gazed at Ellie in awe, then placed lingering kisses on her forehead and cheek before claiming her lips once again. Ellie broke the kiss and pushed Johanna onto her back, then cuddled into her side, her head on Johanna's shoulder.

"You are an incredible lover," Ellie said with a sigh. "How have I survived so long without your touch?"

"And I so long without touching you. My heart is overflowing, my love. I think I've only been half alive, until now."

"Oh, Johanna, I love you so much. I've no idea what the future holds, but I know I want to be by your side, forever."

"As long as I draw breath, I'll love you, Ellie. You are the best thing that's ever happened to me. In you, God gave me my very own ray of sunshine, and you brought my heart back to life. Thank you for not giving up on me."

Tears spilled from Ellie's eyes as she pulled Johanna closer. "And thank you for trusting me with your heart. I promise that you'll never be alone again."

Moments later, Johanna lay still, reveling in the feel of Ellie in her arms.

"While you were away, I signed the lease for the flat we liked. I was afraid I'd be living there without you, but now, I can't wait to move in." When Ellie didn't respond, Johanna's insecurities reared up. *What if she doesn't want to live with me?*

"Ellie?" Johanna looked over to find Ellie sound asleep against her shoulder, and her heart surged with love. She nearly pinched herself, still not believing that this beautiful, intelligent, loving woman was hers. She kissed the top of Ellie's head and whispered, "All of me is yours while my heart beats."

## EPILOGUE

*Spring 1919*

"Papa, I'm so glad you came," Ellie said, as she greeted her father in the vestibule. "Things have progressed splendidly since you were last here."

"Yes, I see," her father said, looking into the spacious, comfortable sitting room where four convalescents sat playing chess. "It looks as if you've done wonders with the place."

"Indeed we have, thanks to you. I don't think we ever would have found such a perfect location, let alone the funds we needed, without you and your contacts."

Ellie's father had made inquiries amongst his friends and colleagues and found this grand, well-kept manor house in Leith. The grounds were stunning, with manicured lawns, gardens, pastureland, and sturdy stables for several horses. In addition, he had told everyone he knew about his daughter's grand idea, and donations had steadily come in.

"It's been my pleasure. I'm so very proud of you."

"Thank you, Papa," Ellie said, kissing his cheek.

"Now come outside. I have a surprise for you."

Ellie's curiosity was piqued as she followed her father out to the circular drive in front of the house. Johanna and Theo stood beside a shiny black horse-drawn hackney carriage. Theo smiled and opened the door, and Ellie just stared. Emerging from the carriage was her mother.

"Hello, Eleanor. Do close your mouth."

"Mother? I can't believe you're here."

"Frankly, neither can I, but if I'm to ever see my children, I suppose I'll have to travel on occasion. Your father insisted I come see your, ah, facility."

Ellie nodded, dumbstruck. Theo laughed and took his mother's arm.

"Mother, I'd like you to meet our dear friend, Johanna Lennox."

Their mother looked Johanna up and down. "So you're the one who drew my children away from home."

Ellie found her voice before Johanna could respond. "Actually, Mother, Theo and I made our choice all by ourselves. Surrey is where we come from, but this is where we belong."

As if sensing Ellie's temper rising, Johanna stepped forward and offered her hand. "It's a pleasure to make your acquaintance, Lady Violet. Your children are wonderful people—you must be so proud."

"Yes, well…Charles, I must get out of the sun. Take me inside."

"Yes, dear," he said, winking behind her back at the other three.

"Well done, Jo," Theo said, "stepping in before Ellie popped her cork."

Johanna grinned. "It's my new mission to win your mother over. Do I stand a chance?"

"You survived a war, so you've a decent chance of surviving our mother," Ellie replied. "We'll soon see if she's gearing up for battle or here to make peace."

Theo laughed and clapped Johanna on the shoulder. "Steady on, soldier, but watch your back."

They went inside to find Fiona Campbell chatting with the Winthrops in the parlor reserved for visitors.

"Yes, Ellie was one of our finest volunteers, and Johanna the best of my nurses. I was thrilled to be invited to work with them again."

"But is this work really suitable for well-bred women?"

"Oh yes," Fiona said, deftly deflecting the veiled insult. "The smartest, most worldly women make the best nurses. Besides, how can helping one's fellow man be anything but a divine calling?"

Fiona had things well in hand, but Ellie was still a bit tetchy.

"Papa, a word?"

She stepped back into the vestibule, and when he joined her, she beckoned him outside.

"Why is she here, Papa? I won't stand for my friends to be insulted."

"Now, Ellie, you know she's just testing them to see what they're made of. Seems to me your friends are passing with flying colors."

"But if she isn't in support of our mission here…"

"Let me tell you something, Ellie. I believe that, in her own way, she has come around. When Theo came home, she was shocked to see his injury, sheltered as she was from the reality of war. When he told us that he wanted to establish a working stable for the residents here, she couldn't understand the need. He took her to see his old schoolmate who was in a convalescent hospital, so that she could see firsthand the physical devastation with which these men must now cope. When they came home, she went to her room and stayed there, weeping, until the next morning. That was the turning point in her attitude, I think."

Ellie, moved by his account, felt her anger slip away. "Thank you for telling me, Papa. I just wish she wasn't so negative."

"Perhaps if you look for the positive, you'll see it, Ellie."

Ellie's cheeks burned from his gentle scolding, and she nodded, vowing to give her mother a chance.

"I wondered where you two had gone," Theo said, joining them. "Papa, I'd like to take you down to the stables, if now's a good time. I've got a fine new stallion I'd like to show off."

Ellie kissed her father on the cheek. "Go on. I think you'll be quite impressed with Theo's work."

"All right then, son, lead the way."

Ellie grew misty-eyed as she watched the two men she loved most walk away. She was blessed to have them and she said yet another prayer of gratitude that Theo had survived the war. After a moment, she went back inside to join the others.

"Ah, there you are," Johanna said, her radiant smile chasing Ellie's clouds away. "We were just telling your mother that it's time for our rounds. Lady Violet, it's been a pleasure. We'll leave you two to catch up."

As they left, Johanna lightly brushed Ellie's arm. "Breathe," she whispered. "I love you."

Ellie smiled, her heart full. She joined her mother, who was seated by the window, looking out at a colorful bed of tulips.

"So, how was your trip?" Ellie said, taking the seat opposite.

"Long and bumpy, but at least the weather held. It's a fine day."

"Yes, it is. Mother, I'm glad you came all this way to visit us."

"You are? I thought perhaps...well, never mind." Her mother sighed and looked away.

Ellie took a deep breath and took the plunge. "Mother, I know we haven't always seen eye to eye, and you perhaps haven't understood or approved of my choices, but it would mean the world to me to have your blessing." There, she'd said it. Ellie sat, hands clasped tightly, and steeled herself for her mother's reaction.

After several tense moments, Mother spoke. "Miss Lennox and Miss Campbell spoke very highly of you, Eleanor. They told me how hard you've worked to establish this home, how tireless and dedicated you are to ensuring its success. You're right, you know. I haven't always understood your choices, and I stubbornly held to the notion that your life should follow the same path as mine. I regret that now."

She looked up at Ellie with tear-filled eyes. "I envy you, Eleanor. You have more courage and conviction in your little finger than I've ever had, and I was a fool not to see it. I'm very proud of you, and I hope you'll forgive me."

Tears spilled down Ellie's cheeks as she rose from her chair. Kneeling beside her mother, she nodded. "I love you, Mama." She laid her head on her mother's knee, rejoicing when she felt a hand gently stroking her hair.

She heard her mother's voice catch on a sob as she replied, "I love you, too, my Ellie."

Johanna and Ellie hadn't had a moment alone to talk until now, as they readied for bed.

"What a day," Ellie said, plopping down on the stool at her dressing table.

"Seemed to turn out better than you expected," Johanna replied, coming to stand behind her. She removed the pins from Ellie's hair and began to brush it. Such little intimacies were the best parts of her day. She watched Ellie's face in the mirror as she closed her eyes and began to relax.

"My mother was full of surprises. Not only was she impressed with you and Fiona, but she said she was proud of me. I've waited years to hear those words."

"Oh, darling, I'm so happy things have worked out between you. I thought your parents were wonderful. I don't think it could've been a more perfect day."

Ellie opened her eyes and gazed at Johanna's reflection. "I can think of one way to top it," she said, pulling her hair aside to reveal her neck.

Johanna smiled and put the brush aside. Accepting the invitation, she kissed Ellie's soft skin, nuzzling the velvety spot beneath her earlobe. She untied the strings at the neck of Ellie's nightgown and eased it off one shoulder, her lips caressing every inch of exposed skin.

"That feels heavenly," Ellie said, reaching up behind her to thread her fingers through Johanna's hair.

"I've only just begun." Johanna grasped Ellie's shoulders and turned her around, then knelt before her. "Have you any idea the joy you bring me, lass?" she said, running her hands along Ellie's thighs. "I need you like I need air."

Ellie cupped Johanna's face in her hands. "Oh, my love, I feel the same. You are everything that's beautiful and good in this world."

She brought Johanna's head to her chest and held her close. Johanna rested her cheek on one breast and brought her hand up to stroke the other. As she circled the nipple through the thin fabric, Ellie's breath quickened. Suddenly she pressed Johanna's shoulders back and stood.

"Bed, now."

Johanna chuckled and got up from her knees, lifting the hem of Ellie's nightgown as she rose. "We can leave this here," she said, sliding the garment over Ellie's head. Standing naked, her porcelain skin flushed and her blue eyes dark with desire, Ellie took Johanna's breath away.

Ellie grasped Johanna's hand and moved to the bed, captured Johanna's lips in a fiery kiss as she undressed her, then stepped back.

"Ah, lass, the way you look at me sets my body on fire."

"I can't help it. You're stunning." Ellie placed a finger on Johanna's lips, then drew a slow and meandering path down her body until she touched the soft curls between her legs. "Sometimes I still can't believe you're mine." Dipping into the wetness there, Ellie moaned. "Lie back and let me love you."

Johanna stretched out on the bed, her body twitching with need, and watched as Ellie knelt between her legs.

"I love your breasts," Ellie said, caressing them and rubbing Johanna's hard nipples.

"I'm very glad you do," Johanna said, biting her lip as pleasure coursed through her. She moaned when Ellie replaced her hands with her mouth, licking and sucking until Johanna could take no more. Her hips came off the bed and Ellie grasped her bottom, nudging Johanna's legs apart as she moved down the bed.

"I'm going to taste you now," Ellie said, her voice husky and low.

Johanna cried out at the first touch of Ellie's tongue, every nerve in her body centered right there, and a wave of heat washed over her. Ellie explored Johanna with her tongue, stroking and tasting as her hands tried to still Johanna's hips. It was no use—the moment Ellie plunged her tongue inside, Johanna lost control. Her hips writhed and bucked as Ellie brought her to the edge and over, her body shuddering with release.

When Johanna could lift her head, she looked for Ellie. Her head was pillowed on Johanna's belly, and her face sported a huge smile.

"You look mighty proud of yourself," Johanna teased.

"Oh, I am," Ellie said. "I was just thinking about all those volunteers who were frightened to death of you back in Boulogne. Do you think they'd believe that I've tamed the fearsome Sister Lennox?" She reached up to tweak a nipple, and Johanna swatted her hand.

"Oh, stop," she said, laughing, but then just as quickly sobered.

"What is it, love? Did I upset you?"

"No…it's just that the tough, no-nonsense Sister Lennox is who I had to become to survive, but I don't need her anymore. You found the real Johanna and brought her back to life. The woman I am with you is who I think I was always meant to be."

Ellie moved up and laid her head on Johanna's shoulder, placing a hand over her heart. "My sweet, sweet love, you saved me from a false and miserable life. Without you, I might never have found the courage to truly be myself."

"Seems we saved each other, then," Johanna said, holding Ellie close.

"Yes, we did. Oh, guess what I found this morning?"

"What?"

"I dropped that volume of Dickinson on the floor when I was dusting the bookshelves, and a poem fell out. It's there on the nightstand."

Johanna reached over for the book and opened it. On a sheet of stationery inside the front cover was a poem she had written, forever ago, it seemed.

"My God, I'd forgotten," she said, embarrassed. "I'm no writer, Ellie. I'm sure it's bloody awful."

Ellie propped herself up on her elbow. "It's beautiful. Read it to me," Ellie said.

Johanna hesitated, then cleared her throat and began.

*While my heart still beats, I will love you*
*While my lungs draw breath, I will need you*
*While my eyes have sight, I will want you*
*While my hands can touch, I will hold you*
*It's my greatest wish and my heartfelt prayer*
*That wherever you are, I too will be there*
*To love you for always and be by your side*
*As the sand is forever caressed by the tide.*

Ellie leaned down and kissed Johanna with all the love her heart could hold. "Always and forever, my darling."

# About the Author

Erin McKenzie has been a lover of words since she first learned her ABCs, sparking a lifelong passion for reading, writing, and of course, word games! She is a professional high school counselor, partner to her wife of eighteen years, Mommy to their three children, chief dishwasher and laundry folder, soccer mom and homework checker. Her happy places are the beach or deep within the pages of a good book...preferably both at once. She and her family live in the Finger Lakes region of New York State and share their home with several beloved fur babies.

Erin is the author of *Where Love Leads*, *Taking Chances*, and her first foray into historical romance, *While My Heart Beats*.

# Books Available from Bold Strokes Books

**Everyday People** by Louis Barr. When Film star Diana Danning hires private eye Clint Steele to find her son, Clint turns to his former West Point barracks mate, and ex-buddy with benefits, Mars Hauser to lend his cyber espionage and digital black ops skills to the case. (978-1-63555-698-8)

**Forging a Desire Line** by Mary P. Burns. When Charley's ex-wife, Tricia, is diagnosed with inoperable cancer, the private duty nurse Tricia hires turns out to be the handsome and aloof Joanna, who ignites something inside Charley she isn't ready to face. (978-1-63555-665-0)

**Love on the Night Shift** by Radclyffe. Between ruling the night shift in the ER at the Rivers and raising her teenage daughter, Blaise Richilieu has all the drama she needs in her life, until a dashing young attending appears on the scene and relentlessly pursues her. (978-1-63555-668-1)

**Olivia's Awakening** by Ronica Black. When the daring and dangerously gorgeous Eve Monroe is hired to get Olivia Savage into shape, a fierce passion ignites, causing both to question everything they've ever known about love. (978-1-63555-613-1)

**The Duchess and the Dreamer** by Jenny Frame. Clementine Fitzroy has lost her faith and love of life. Can dreamer Evan Fox make her believe in life and dream again? (978-1-63555-601-8)

**The Road Home** by Erin Zak. Hollywood actress Gwendolyn Carter is about to discover that losing someone you love sometimes means gaining someone to fall for. (978-1-63555-633-9)

**Waiting for You** by Elle Spencer. When passionate past-life lovers meet again in the present day, one remembers it vividly and the other isn't so sure. (978-1-63555-635-3)

**While My Heart Beats** by Erin McKenzie. Can a love born amidst the horrors of the Great War survive? (978-1-63555-589-9)

**Face the Music** by Ali Vali. Sweet music is the last thing that happens when Nashville music producer Mason Liner, and daughter of country royalty Victoria Roddy are thrown together in an effort to save country star Sophie Roddy's career. (978-1-63555-532-5)

**Flavor of the Month** by Georgia Beers. What happens when baker Charlie and chef Emma realize their differing paths have led them right back to each other? (978-1-63555-616-2)

**Mending Fences** by Angie Williams. Rancher Bobbie Del Rey and veterinarian Grace Hammond are about to discover if heartbreaks of the past can ever truly be mended. (978-1-63555-708-4)

**Silk and Leather: Lesbian Erotica with an Edge** edited by Victoria Villasenor. This collection of stories by award winning authors offers fantasies as soft as silk and tough as leather. The only question is: How far will you go to make your deepest desires come true? (978-1-63555-587-5)

**The Last Place You Look** by Aurora Rey. Dumped by her wife and looking for anything but love, Julia Pierce retreats to her hometown, only to rediscover high school friend Taylor Winslow, who's secretly crushed on her for years. (978-1-63555-574-5)

**The Mortician's Daughter** by Nan Higgins. A singer on the verge of stardom discovers she must give up her dreams to live a life in service to ghosts. (978-1-63555-594-3)

**The Real Thing** by Laney Webber. When passion flares between actress Virginia Green and masseuse Allison McDonald, can they be sure it's the real thing? (978-1-63555-478-6)

**What the Heart Remembers Most** by M. Ullrich. For college sweethearts Jax Levine and Gretchen Mills, could an accident be the second chance neither knew they wanted? (978-1-63555-401-4)

**White Horse Point** by Andrews & Austin. Mystery writer Taylor James finds herself falling for the mysterious woman on White Horse Point who lives alone, protecting a secret she can't share about a murderer who walks among them. (978-1-63555-695-7)

**Femme Tales** by Anne Shade. Six women find themselves in their own real-life fairy tales when true love finds them in the most unexpected ways. (978-1-63555-657-5)

**Jellicle Girl** by Stevie Mikayne. One dark summer night, Beth and Jackie go out to the canoe dock. Two years later, Beth is still carrying the weight of what happened to Jackie. (978-1-63555-691-9)

**Le Berceau** by Julius Eks. If only Ben could tear his heart in two, then he wouldn't have to choose between the love of his life and the most beautiful boy he has ever seen. (978-1-63555-688-9)

**My Date with a Wendigo** by Genevieve McCluer. Elizabeth Rosseau finds her long lost love and the secret community of fiends she's now a part of. (978-1-63555-679-7)

**On the Run** by Charlotte Greene. Even when they're cute blondes, it's stupid to pick up hitchhikers, especially when they've just broken out of prison, but doing so is about to change Gwen's life forever. (978-1-63555-682-7)

**Perfect Timing** by Dena Blake. The choice between love and family has never been so difficult, and Lynn's and Maggie's different visions of the future may end their romance before it's begun. (978-1-63555-466-3)

**The Mail Order Bride** by R Kent. When a mail order bride is thrust on Austin, he must choose between the bride he never wanted or the dream he lives for. (978-1-63555-678-0)

**Through Love's Eyes** by C.A. Popovich. When fate reunites Brittany Yardin and Amy Jansons, can they move beyond the pain of their past to find love? (978-1-63555-629-2)

**To the Moon and Back** by Melissa Brayden. Film actress Carly Daniel thinks that stage work is boring and unexciting, but when she accepts a lead role in a new play, stage manager Lauren Prescott tests both her heart and her ability to share the limelight. (978-1-63555-618-6)

**Tokyo Love** by Diana Jean. When Kathleen Schmitt is given the opportunity to be on the cutting edge of AI technology, she never thought a failed robotic love companion would bring her closer to her neighbor, Yuriko Velucci, and finding love in unexpected places. (978-1-63555-681-0)

**Brooklyn Summer** by Maggie Cummings. When opposites attract, can a summer of passion and adventure lead to a lifetime of love? (978-1-63555-578-3)

**City Kitty and Country Mouse** by Alyssa Linn Palmer. Pulled in two different directions, can a city kitty and country mouse fall in love and make it work? (978-1-63555-553-0)

**Elimination** by Jackie D. When a dangerous homegrown terrorist seeks refuge with the Russian mafia, the team will be put to the ultimate test. (978-1-63555-570-7)

**In the Shadow of Darkness** by Nicole Stiling. Angeline Vallencourt is a reluctant vampire who must decide what she wants more—obscurity, revenge, or the woman who makes her feel alive. (978-1-63555-624-7)

**On Second Thought** by C. Spencer. Madisen is falling hard for Rae. Even single life and co-parenting are beginning to click. At least, that is, until her ex-wife begins to have second thoughts. (978-1-63555-415-1)

**Out of Practice** by Carsen Taite. When attorney Abby Keane discovers the wedding blogger tormenting her client is the woman she had a passionate, anonymous vacation fling with, sparks and subpoenas fly. Legal Affairs: one law firm, three best friends, three chances to fall in love. (978-1-63555-359-8)

**Providence** by Leigh Hays. With every click of the shutter, photographer Rebekiah Kearns finds it harder and harder to keep Lindsey Blackwell in focus without getting too close. (978-1-63555-620-9)

**Taking a Shot at Love** by KC Richardson. When academic and athletic worlds collide, will English professor Celeste Bouchard and basketball coach Lisa Tobias ignore their attraction to achieve their professional goals? (978-1-63555-549-3)

**Flight to the Horizon** by Julie Tizard. Airline captain Kerri Sullivan and flight attendant Janine Case struggle to survive an emergency water landing and overcome dark secrets to give love a chance to fly. (978-1-63555-331-4)

**In Helen's Hands** by Nanisi Barrett D'Arnuk. As her mistress, Helen pushes Mickey to her sensual limits, delivering the pleasure only a BDSM lifestyle can provide her. (978-1-63555-639-1)

**Jamis Bachman, Ghost Hunter** by Jen Jensen. In Sage Creek, Utah, a poltergeist stirs to life and past secrets emerge. (978-1-63555-605-6)

**Moon Shadow** by Suzie Clarke. Add betrayal, season with survival, then serve revenge smokin' hot with a sharp knife. (978-1-63555-584-4)

**Spellbound** by Jean Copeland and Jackie D. When the supernatural worlds of good and evil face off, love might be what saves them all. (978-1-63555-564-6)

**Temptation** by Kris Bryant. Can experienced nanny Cassie Miller deny her growing attraction and keep her relationship with her boss professional? Or will they sidestep propriety and give in to temptation? (978-1-63555-508-0)

**The Inheritance** by Ali Vali. Family ties bring Tucker Delacroix and Willow Vernon together, but they could also tear them, and any chance they have at love, apart. (978-1-63555-303-1)

**Thief of the Heart** by MJ Williamz. Kit Hanson makes a living seducing rich women in casinos and relieving them of the expensive jewelry most won't even miss. But her streak ends when she meets beautiful FBI agent Savannah Brown. (978-1-63555-572-1)